Kathy's New Brother

Best Friends

#6

Kathy's New Brother

Hilda Stahl

CROSSWAY BOOKS • WHEATON, ILLINOIS
A DIVISION OF GOOD NEWS PUBLISHERS

Dedicated with love to
Kathy Jacobs
Thanks for your help
and your friendship

Kathy's New Brother.

Copyright © 1992 by Word Spinners, Inc.

Published by Crossway Books, a division of
Good News Publishers, 1300 Crescent Street, Wheaton, Illinois 60187.

Cover illustration: Paul Casale

First printing, 1992

Printed in the United States of America

Library of Congress Cataloging-in-Publication Data
Stahl, Hilda.
　　Kathy's new brother / Hilda Stahl.
　　　　p.　　cm. — (Best friends : #6)
　　Summary: With the help of her faith and her friends, sixth-grader
Kathy learns to accept her foster brother and the trouble-making girl on
the cheerleading squad that Kathy wants to join.
　　　[1. Friendship—Fiction.　2. Brothers and sisters—Fiction.
3. Foster home care—Fiction.　4. Christian life—Fiction.]
I. Title.　II. Series: Stahl, Hilda.　Best friends : #6.
PZ7.S78244Kau 1992　　　　[Fic]—dc20　　　　　　92-9135
ISBN 0-89107-682-4

00		99		98		97		96		95		94		93		92
15	14	13	12	11	10	9	8	7	6	5	4	3	2	1

Contents

1

Good News

Smiling such a big smile she thought her face would crack, Kathy stood in the shade of Chelsea's backyard with Hannah and Roxie and listened to Chelsea tell every detail of how she'd finally paid off her huge phone bill. When she finished, Kathy caught Chelsea's hands and twirled around with her. "Way to go, Chel! Congratulations!"

"Thanks!" Chelsea tipped back her red head and laughed. "I never thought this day would come!"

Her black eyes sparkling, Hannah lifted Chelsea's freckled arm high in victory. "You're free of debt at last!"

"You said you'd do it, and you did!" Roxie lifted Chelsea's other arm.

"I never thought I'd ever have money to spend again!" Her long red hair streaming out behind her, Chelsea danced across her backyard, then danced back. When she'd moved from Oklahoma to The Ravines in Middle Lake, Michigan, she'd called her best friend every day and had built up a terrible phone bill. She'd paid it herself by starting a business, along with Roxie, Hannah, and Kathy, called the *King's Kids*. It was called that because they all belonged to Jesus. They did odd jobs around the neighborhood. Some of the other kids who lived in The Ravines helped. It was a very profitable business.

Wiping sweat off her short cap of dark hair, Roxie dropped to the grass in the shade of a tall maple. "It's too hot to get this excited."

"You're right," the others agreed, laughing.

Brushing sweat off her face, Kathy sat on the grass between Hannah and Chelsea and across from Roxie. They all wore shorts and T-shirts with *I'm A Best Friend* buttons pinned in place. Kathy smelled the sweet aroma of purple flowers. A hot August wind fluttered the leaves in the trees between Chelsea's house and Roxie's. Hannah lived directly across the street from Chelsea. Kathy pulled her knees to her chin and closed her hazel eyes for a moment. Sometimes she wished she lived in The Ravines too, instead of across the street from the subdivision in an older section of Middle Lake. It would be fun to live closer to the Best Friends.

Smiling, Hannah nudged Kathy on the leg. "I

saw your dad on TV last night. He plays the guitar sooo well!"

"Thanks." Kathy was proud that Dad was the lead musician on a Christian talk show. He'd worked hard at his music as long as she could remember.

"I'd love to be able to play guitar." Chelsea sighed a loud, long sigh. "But it takes too much practice. And my fingers hurt when I tried."

"Everything takes practice." Roxie flexed her fingers. "If I don't use my carving tools to carve something, I have to practice again just to make the knives do what I want."

"I sure like the raccoon you're working on now." Kathy leaned forward eagerly. She wished she could be the artist Roxie was, but she knew she couldn't. Roxie had a special gift. "Did you get it finished yet?"

"No. I guess we've been too busy talking about the wedding." Roxie rolled her eyes. "Grandma Potter and Ezra Menski really are getting married . . . September first . . . And that's only a week away!"

"And then school starts," Chelsea whispered with a shiver.

Kathy pushed her fingers back and forth in her thick blonde curls. They were damp and tight. She wished her hair was smooth and long and easy to brush. "I really don't mind that school's starting.

But you won't believe who'll be going to middle school with us."

"Who?" the others asked together.

Kathy scowled. "Brody Vangaar!"

"What's wrong with that?" Hannah asked as she pushed her long black hair over her shoulder. "I thought you liked Brody."

"He's all right, I guess." Kathy sighed heavily. "It's just that he's *always* at our house! Dad said he'd help him since his dad is gone and his brother's in jail for dealing drugs, but that doesn't mean he has to hang around all the time. It's almost like I have two brothers instead of just one! And now he'll even be going to the same school!"

"But not in sixth grade like us," Roxie said. "He'll be in seventh, won't he?"

Kathy nodded.

Chelsea looked at her watch. "We'd better have our *King's Kids* meeting before it's time for y'all to go home." She took a deep breath. "Let's take a vote whether to keep on with *King's Kids* or drop it."

"The extra money is nice," Hannah said.

Kathy thought of the baby she watched every Monday evening and the two lawns she mowed. She had used the money to help buy school clothes. "I don't want to give up my jobs."

"We could work on Saturdays and maybe one day after school," Roxie said.

Smiling, Chelsea nodded. "Good idea! I saw

some really cute jeans I want to buy, and they cost way too much to get with just my allowance." She looked at the others. "Raise your hand if you vote to continue with *King's Kids* on Saturdays and one night a week."

Kathy raised her hand along with the others. "I might have to watch Megan some Saturdays though." Megan was four, and because both Kathy's parents worked, she and Duke took turns watching her.

"We'll work around that," Chelsea said. "All of us have to baby-sit younger brothers or sisters once in a while." She rolled her eyes. "I'll be glad when Mike is old enough to watch himself!"

"It'll be years before my baby brother is old enough to watch himself." Suddenly Hannah laughed. "I'll be in college before he can take care of himself! College!"

Roxie bit her lip. "Sometimes it scares me to think about college. I might get lonely living in a dorm. And maybe I won't be smart enough to pass the classes. You have to be really smart to go to college."

Hannah clasped her hands together. "Why don't we all go to the same college?" Her face fell. "Maybe that won't work. I'm Ottawa, and I might not be able to get into the same school you girls want to go to."

"People aren't as prejudiced against Native Americans as they used to be," Chelsea said.

"Even a little hurts," Hannah whispered.

Kathy nodded. "I know how bad it hurt when people thought my dad did drugs just because he had long hair, dressed funny, and is a musician. They don't say that since he cut his hair and dresses in nice clothes. And he's still the same person!"

"You can't judge others by what they look like." Roxie giggled. "That's what my dad always says. Especially if I get embarrassed when he wears dirty overalls to the grocery store."

"I might go back to Oklahoma for college," Chelsea said in her Oklahoma accent. "Rob said he might too." He was her older brother, and he was an expert with his computer.

"We could all go there!" Hannah cried. "Wouldn't that be exciting?"

Kathy thought about leaving her family, and a shiver ran down her spine. "I don't think I could leave Michigan."

"Me either." Roxie shook her head.

Chelsea grinned and shrugged. "We still have a long time before we have to decide."

Kathy sighed in relief. She wasn't ready to think about college.

Several minutes later Kathy jumped up and ran to her bike. "I'll see you tomorrow," she said over her shoulder. The Best Friends got together almost every day. Kathy liked that. She could talk to them about *anything* and they'd understand and help if they could. She pedaled away from Chelsea's house and down the shady street to the end of The Ravines. Kids played in almost every yard. She crossed the street to Kennedy Street where she'd lived in the four-bedroom brick house all her eleven years. It would feel strange to move.

Just before she reached her house she saw Alyssa Carroll and three other girls practicing cheerleading. Kathy stopped her bike and watched them jump and twirl and shout. The sound filled the yard. The girls were all the same height and size, and all wore yellow T-shirts and blue shorts. They looked great together. Kathy sighed heavily. How she wished she could be a cheerleader! She'd taken lessons with all four of the girls and knew every move. She was good too! Then she'd had to take care of Megan on practice day and had had to drop the lessons. She practiced at home in her backyard regularly, but it wasn't the same as doing it with the group.

She watched them together, then one at a time—Alyssa Carroll, Debbie Ellison, Justine Gold, and Sharon Warrick. "And Kathy Aber," she whispered. Even as she said her name she remembered Alyssa making fun of her last name. It was pronounced A-bear, so Alyssa called her A Teddy Bear to make her angry. She shrugged. Even though Alyssa liked to tease her about her name, Kathy wanted to be a cheerleader.

Her legs weak, she wheeled her bike into Alyssa's yard. A butterfly fluttered around tall blue flowers. A robin flew to the ground, then flew away. Kathy waited until the girls finished the cheer. "Hi. You're looking good."

"Thanks." Alyssa smiled slightly.

"Hi," the others said.

"Can I do a cheer with you?" Kathy's stomach knotted. Why had she even asked? They were sure to say no. Quickly she added, "I guess I'd better not stay. I have to get home."

"Are you going to try out for the team this year?" Justine asked. Her dark blonde hair was pulled back in a long ponytail. Her hazel eyes looked large and pretty in her oval face.

"I'd like to."

"You can practice with us if you want," Debbie said.

"Thanks!"

Alyssa frowned at Debbie. "We have to vote on it."

"Oh, that's right." Debbie's face turned red. "I vote yes."

Kathy bit her lip to hold back a cry. Would they vote against her and embarrass her? "Never mind. It's no big deal." But it *was* a big deal! She really wanted to practice with them. She wouldn't walk away without knowing. She took a deep breath. "Sure . . . Go ahead and vote."

14

Raising dark brows over her bright blue eyes, Alyssa looked at the girls. "Well?"

"Yes," they all three said.

Kathy sighed in relief. Her legs trembled, and she leaned against her bike to keep from tumbling into the grass.

Alyssa shrugged. "I guess you can practice with us. We meet every afternoon at 2. Can you make it?"

Kathy nodded. She'd find a way.

"We're done for today, so we'll see you tomorrow." Alyssa crossed her arms. "We always meet in *my* yard."

"You're welcome to come to mine," Kathy said. "We have a big backyard."

Alyssa frowned. "We *always* meet in mine!"

Kathy flushed. "Well, okay, I'll come here." She wanted to ask Alyssa why it always had to be her way, but she didn't dare. Alyssa might make the girls vote against letting her practice with them. "See you tomorrow at 2."

"Bye." Justine smiled and lifted her hand in a wave. Debbie and Sharon just smiled. Alyssa didn't do anything.

Smiling even though she had a knot in her stomach, Kathy pedaled home. They had voted to let her practice with them! With a shaky laugh Kathy put her bike in the garage and ran into the house. She found Mom in the living room drinking a tall glass of water and watching a Gospel Bill video with Megan. The window air conditioner cooled the room. Mom looked up and smiled. Laugh lines spread from the corners of her dark brown eyes to her short brown hair. She wore a loose-fitting light blue blouse over matching shorts and tan sandals. Megan sat close beside her, but didn't take her eyes off the television.

Mom pushed herself up and walked over to Kathy. "What's up? You look ready to burst."

"I talked to Alyssa and the other cheerleaders, and they're going to let me practice with them."

"That's great!"

Kathy bit her lip. Maybe it wasn't so great after all. "Every day at 2."

"Oh." Mom glanced at Megan, then shrugged. "We'll work it out. I know how much you want to be a cheerleader."

Kathy smiled. "Thanks, Mom! I guess I'll have to get a yellow T-shirt and blue shorts like they all have."

"We could go this evening. I have a couple of things to pick up for your dad. Now that he's on TV regularly, he needs more clothes than when he stayed at home and gave music lessons." Mom grinned. "But it's worth it."

Kathy touched her *I'm A Best Friend* button. Wait'll she told the others her great news! She frowned thoughtfully. Would they be happy for her?

2

The Terrible News

Kathy poured cold milk on her bowl of raisin bran just as Dad walked in for breakfast. He stretched and yawned, then pulled his T-shirt down over his faded denim shorts. His white T-shirt said, "Jesus the Solid Rock" in red on the front of it. It hung loose on his bony body.

"Morning, Kit Kat."

"Hi." Kathy smiled. It sometimes embarrassed her to have Dad call her by that pet name, but today it made her feel warm all over. "Want some raisin bran?"

"Sure." Dad pulled a glass bowl from the cupboard and filled it with cereal and milk. He drizzled honey over it, sat down, and took a bite. "What's going on with you today?"

Kathy smiled. "At 2 I'm going to practice cheerleading! I bought my yellow T-shirt and blue shorts last night."

"I don't suppose the shirt and jeans you're wearing now would work."

"Oh, Dad." Kathy shook her head. She knew Dad didn't think clothes were important like other people did. "It's like a uniform."

"Don't ever be afraid to think for yourself, Kathleen. It's important to be clean and tidy, but you don't have to follow the crowd in order to be somebody. You're somebody because God made man—and you—in His image. You're valuable and important. Don't let anybody say you're not just because you might not act or think or look like everybody else."

"Okay, Dad." Kathy took a bit of cereal. She liked the sweet taste of the raisins, the crunch of the flakes, and the feel of the cold milk. She knew Dad was right, but she didn't think she was following the crowd too much. She was still thinking for herself, wasn't she?

"Has Duke had breakfast already?" Dad asked.

Kathy shrugged. "I didn't see him."

"Brody's coming early today. He called late last night to tell us."

Kathy gripped her spoon. "Dad, does he have to be here all the time?"

"If that's what it takes to help him, yes." Dad studied Kathy with narrowed blue eyes. "You said that was OK when we asked how you felt about our helping him."

"I know. It's just that sometimes it feels like he *lives* here."

"It would be better for him if he did."

"But not for me!" Kathy wanted to say, but she didn't. Dad would tell her she needed to ask Jesus to help her love Brody with *His* love. She didn't want to do that. It was enough that she'd voted for the family to help Brody. He didn't need her to love him!

Dad ate in silence for a while. "I've talked to his mom about letting him come here to live, but she won't allow it. I know I'd never give you or Megan or Duke up, so I understand how she feels. But I told her that if the situation makes it necessary, she should let us sort of take him into our family and be legally responsible for him."

"That won't happen."

"I suppose not." Dad leaned back in his chair. "Another week and school starts. Sixth grade. Are you excited?"

"I guess. I'll be glad when I'm in high school."

"Don't wish away your life, Kathy. Time goes fast enough as it is."

"Not to me."

"Think about it—just yesterday you were a baby, and now you're eleven, almost twelve."

Kathy smiled. "And then thirteen! A teenager, Dad!"

"Kit Kat, I want you to stay young a while longer. I like you just the age you are. But next year I'll like you that age too." Dad grinned. "Unless you suddenly change into a monster like I've heard some parents say happened to their teenagers."

Kathy giggled. "I've heard that some *parents* turn into monsters when their kids become teenagers."

Dad reached across the table and tweaked Kathy's chin. "I will never become a monster." Suddenly he jumped up, roared, ran around the table, and grabbed her. He nibbled on her ear and growled again.

Kathy laughed and tried to pull away. "Daddy, you're silly."

"But you love me anyway."

She kissed his cheek. "Yep."

Just then the doorbell rang. Duke shouted that he'd answer it.

Kathy hurried to the hall with Dad close behind her. Maybe the Best Friends were coming to visit!

Duke opened the door, and Brody stepped inside, his guitar slung over his back and two bags in his hands. He set them down and just stood there. His shirt and jeans looked as if he'd slept in them, and his hair was oily and uncombed.

Kathy stared at him in shock. Her heart zoomed to her feet. Did this mean Brody was moving in? Oh, it couldn't be!

"Hi," Duke said hesitantly. He glanced at Dad, then back to Brody.

Dad stepped forward, his brow raised. "What's up, Brody?"

Brody swallowed hard and looked as if he were going to start crying. "Mom lost her job, and Grandma had a heart attack. So Mom sent me to stay with you." Brody thrust an envelope at Dad. "Mom said she made it legal for you to keep me. She tried to call you but couldn't get through. She had to leave real early this morning for Dallas so she could be with Grandma."

Kathy leaned weakly against the wall. This was the very worst day in her entire life. Brody was actually moving in! He was now her foster brother! She watched Duke and Dad welcome Brody happily. She pressed her lips together and knotted her fists. Just then Brody glanced at her. His face turned red, and he looked quickly away. Had he read her mind? Did he know she didn't want him? Kathy shrugged. So what if he did know? She didn't care.

"Duke, take Brody to your room and get him settled in. I'll tell your mom."

Kathy watched them walk toward the hall that led to the bedrooms. Slowly she walked to the kitchen and sank down in her chair. How would it be to have Brody around all the time?

Just then Megan ran into the room. She wore a flowered sundress and white sandals. Her light brown hair was held in two ponytails by wide green bands. "Guess what? Brody's coming to live with us! He's our brother now. I'm glad. Aren't you glad, Kathy?"

She wanted to shout no, but she couldn't do that to Megan. "If you're happy, I'm happy."

"Me and Natalie are both happy."

Kathy bit back a sharp retort. Megan had given up her make-believe friend twice already. Why did she keep bringing her back? "Want some cereal, Megan?"

"Sure." Megan picked a spoon out of the drawer and a napkin from the counter. She was too short to reach the bowls. She sat at her spot at the table. "I want Cheerios. No, wait! I want Life. No . . . oatmeal."

Kathy rolled her eyes. "Make up your mind, Megan."

"What did you have?"

"Raisin bran."

"I'll have that."

"Are you sure?"

"Shall we, Natalie?" Megan waited, then nodded. "We'll have raisin bran. But don't make a bowl for Natalie. She's on a diet."

Kathy fixed the cereal for Megan and poured her a small glass of orange juice too. Kathy started to unload the dishwasher just as Brody and Duke walked in. Brody was talking to Duke about a song they had been practicing on guitar. He stopped mid-sentence when he saw Kathy. She saw the red stain creep up his neck and over his face. He turned abruptly away.

"I really don't want anything to eat," he said in a low, tight voice.

"Sure, you do." Duke pulled out two bowls. "We can't practice on empty stomachs."

Kathy rushed out of the kitchen and stopped just outside the door. Brody hated her! He hated being in the same room with her! But why? She pressed her hand over her thundering heart and tried to stop trembling. It felt terrible to have him hate her. She heard him talking again, this time to Megan. He sounded kind, and he didn't mumble at all like he did when she was in the same room with him.

"Want me to get you anything else, Megan?"

"No thanks, Brody. Can I listen to you practice?"

"Sure . . . If it's all right with Duke."

"Fine with me."

"I want to play guitar. But I got to wait 'til my fingers are longer, Daddy says. Will my fingers ever be as long as yours, Brody?"

"Sure. Won't they, Duke?"

"Sure." Duke laughed. "Unless you stop growing too soon."

Kathy took a deep breath. She would not stand

outside the kitchen and listen to them talk! She had to get her work done. If Brody couldn't talk with her around, too bad. She took another deep breath and walked back into the kitchen to finish unloading the dishwasher. Brody didn't say another word unless Duke asked him a question he had to answer. Kathy couldn't bring herself to look at him. She didn't want to see him turn red or see the hatred in his eyes.

She finished emptying the dishwasher, then loaded in the few dirty bowls, spoons, and glasses. She tied the plastic garbage bag shut and put a new one in the wastebasket. She carried the full one to the back porch. Later she'd put it out for garbage pickup. If she took it out too soon, the dogs in the neighborhood would tear it open and spread it all over the yard. She stepped back into the kitchen. Brody choked on a bite, then coughed until Duke slapped him on the back.

"Megan, are you ready to go to the park?" Kathy asked, forcing her voice to sound normal.

Megan ran to Kathy. "Ready. Can Brody and Duke come too?"

"They want to practice."

Megan ran to Brody. "Want to go to the park with us?"

He flushed scarlet. "Another time maybe."

Megan hugged his arm. "I love you, Brody." She ran to Duke and did the same thing, then ran to Kathy. "I'm ready to go."

"Tell Mom we left, will you, Duke?" Kathy asked stiffly.

Duke nodded as he spooned another bite into his mouth.

In relief Kathy walked outdoors with Megan. The air was pleasantly cool this early in the day. The smell of baking bread drifted from the house behind theirs. Birds sang in the trees. In the distance a truck roared down the highway.

"I'm glad Brody's our brother now," Megan said as she skipped along beside Kathy. "He tells good stories. And he likes to watch *Cinderella* with me."

Kathy frowned. "He never watched it with you."

Megan stopped short. "He did too!"

Kathy shook her head. She couldn't imagine Brody taking time to watch a video with Megan. She was probably making it up, just like she made up Natalie.

At the park Megan ran to the sandbox, where two girls and a boy were already playing. Kathy sat on a green bench and watched pigeons pecking at potato chips someone had scattered around. Two girls Kathy didn't know ran to the swings. Three boys rode up on bikes, then ran to the field to hit a softball. It was still early, and not many people were at the park. Sometimes Roxie brought Faye. She and Megan were the same age and had fun together.

Hannah had eight-year-old twin sisters and a nine-year-old sister that she sometimes brought to the park. They didn't like playing with Megan or Faye. Chelsea didn't have a sister—only an eight-year-old and a twelve-year-old brother.

Kathy sighed with boredom and twisted the toe of her sneaker in the grass. She should've brought a book to read or maybe the crossword puzzle book she'd been working in.

Why did Brody hate her? Did he know she didn't want him around all the time? He couldn't read her mind.

She jumped up, startling a pigeon. It fluttered to the wishing well and sat on the roof. Why did Brody hate her? She barely spoke to him, so it couldn't be that she'd said something to make him mad at her.

She stamped her foot. "Oh, stop thinking about him!"

Flushing, she glanced around to make sure nobody had heard her. Nobody had, and she breathed easier.

Just then she saw Justine Gold walk into the park. She was alone. Kathy had never seen Justine without the other cheerleaders with her. Kathy waved and called, "Justine!"

Justine flipped back her long, dark blonde hair, hesitated, then ran to Kathy. "Hi. What are you doing here?"

"I brought my little sister to play."

"Oh." Justine looked around. "Is that her in the sandbox?"

"Yes . . . The one in the flowered sundress. How about you?"

Justine shrugged. "I like to walk in the mornings."

Kathy studied Justine. She looked nervous and upset. "Is something wrong?"

"Should there be?"

"I guess not."

Justine perched on the edge of the bench. "Are you ready for school to start?"

"I guess." Kathy sat beside Justine. "Are you?"

"The summer seemed so short!"

"It did to me too. I worked at odd jobs and watched Megan. What did you do?"

"Stayed home . . . Practiced cheerleading." Justine plucked at her blue blouse. "I don't know."

Kathy didn't know what to say. She could see something was bothering Justine, but she didn't know her well enough to ask more. She could do that with the Best Friends, but not with Justine.

"Do you ever get tired of the same old thing, Kathy?"

"Sure."

Justine looked down at the ground. "Like listening to your parents argue?"

"Mine don't argue much."

"You're lucky." Justine bit her lower lip. "Mine do a lot, and then they want me to take sides. I don't want to take sides!"

"I wouldn't either." Kathy moved restlessly. It felt strange to have Justine tell her about her private life.

"I want them to quit fighting, and I've told them that, but it doesn't do any good." Justine spread her hands, then dropped them in her lap. "They just keep on fighting."

"That's too bad." Kathy wanted to say something to help Justine. "Do you pray for them?"

Justine frowned. "I never thought to do that."

"God answers prayer, and He cares about us."

Justine was quiet a long time. "I don't know how to pray."

"Prayer is just talking to God." Smiling, Kathy turned toward Justine. "Did you ever ask Jesus to be your personal Savior?"

"When I was little. It was so long ago I almost forgot about it."

"Jesus is your Friend—your Best Friend. He wants to help you."

Justine wiped a tear off her lashes. "I guess I should start going to church again."

Kathy nodded. "Even if you don't, you can pray and read your Bible. Going to church does help you to remember to do that. And you hear preaching and teaching about Jesus."

"Could I sit with you if I go to your church?"

Kathy thought about making room for Justine with the Best Friends beside her. Finally she nodded. The Best Friends would be glad to see Justine in church and Sunday school.

Justine took a deep breath and brushed at her eyes again. "Will you be at practice today?"

"Yes. It'll be great to do the cheers with a group. I even bought a yellow T-shirt and blue shorts so I'd match."

"You didn't have to do that. We only did because Alyssa said to. She gets really bossy sometimes."

"That's too bad."

"But we put up with it because we want to be cheerleaders." Justine jumped up. "I gotta get going. See you this afternoon."

"See ya."

Justine smiled. "Thanks for your help."

"Glad to." Kathy watched Justine run out of the park. It felt good to help Justine. Kathy leaned back. Too bad someone couldn't help her get rid of Brody. She flushed at the terrible thought. She didn't exactly want to get rid of him. Or did she?

3

Practice

After lunch Kathy leaned against Hannah's bed and listened to her read the Scripture for the day. They'd all agreed that each day they met they'd have a special Bible verse. It was Hannah's turn today to give it.

"Ephesians 2:10. 'For we are God's workmanship, created in Christ Jesus to do good works, which God prepared in advance for us to do.'" Hannah smiled. "Isn't that awesome? We are created in God's image! And He has a special work for us to do."

Kathy remembered that Dad had said at breakfast that she was important because God had made her in His image. Not only was she made in God's image, but He had something special for her to do! She pulled her knees to her chin and looked at the Best Friends on the bed. "I wonder what God wants me to do. Will I have to wait until I'm grown-up to find out?"

Chelsea shook her head. "My dad doesn't think so. He said helping others is one thing God has for *all* of us to do."

Hannah sighed heavily. "I don't get tired of helping others, but sometimes I wish somebody would help me."

"How?" Roxie asked.

Hannah twisted a strand of dark hair around her finger. "I wish someone would convince everyone that Native Americans are people just like other people. So are blacks and Hispanics and Asians. Too many people think that if you're not white, you're just not important."

"We could start an ad campaign to let everyone know we are all equal in God's eyes." Chelsea nodded with a laugh. "We could write it on the back of all of our *King's Kids* flyers! How would that be, Hannah?"

"I don't think that would work." Hannah giggled. "And it might embarrass me, knowing we sent out ads so people would like me better."

"I wish you would all help me with Brody Vangaar." Kathy twisted her fingers together. "He came to live with us today, and I don't know how to act around him."

"He actually came to live with you?" Roxie

asked in surprise. "He just walked in without any warning?"

"Almost." Kathy told the girls what Brody had told her dad. "Brody doesn't like me, and I've decided I don't like him!"

"What makes you think he doesn't like you?" Hannah asked.

"From the way he acts! It's terrible!"

"Maybe he's shy around you because he thinks you don't like him." Hannah pulled her pillow onto her lap and hugged it. "Sometimes people think that about me. Because I'm Ottawa some folks are afraid to treat me like they do others, and then if I don't act or talk just the way they think I should, they think I don't like them. And it's not even true! I just don't want to push myself on someone who doesn't like me. Brody might be feeling that way."

"I don't think so." Kathy jumped up. "I don't want to talk about Brody anymore. I have some really great news!" She waited until they were all looking at her in anticipation. "I am going to do cheerleading with the girls I took lessons with before I had to watch Megan. They practice every afternoon at 2, and I'll be practicing with them."

Hannah smiled. "That's great!"

"What about when school starts?" Roxie asked.

"We'll practice a different time then."

Chelsea's eyes sparkled as she leaned toward Kathy. "Could we watch you practice?"

"Sure." Kathy twirled around. There was plenty of room now that Hannah had her bedroom in the basement. "I want to be a cheerleader this year, and if I practice enough I should make it."

"Ask Mike to help you learn tumbles and flips," Chelsea said. Mike was an expert in gymnastics. "He likes to show off what he knows."

"I'll do that!" Kathy spun around, then stopped so she was facing the girls. "Do you know Justine Gold?"

"Sure," Roxie said. "She's a nice girl—and smart too."

Hannah frowned. "I think I do. Why?"

"She's one of the cheerleaders. She was upset because her mom and dad fight all the time." Kathy's stomach knotted. Justine had probably told her that in confidence, and she'd just blurted it out. What would Justine say if she learned Chelsea, Hannah, and Roxie knew about her parents? Kathy licked her dry lips. "I guess I'd better get home. Practice is at 2 in case you girls want to watch." Kathy shivered. "But not today, okay? It's my first time, and I might mess up if you were watching." And they might say something to Justine about her parents.

"We'll hide behind a tree and sneak a peek." Roxie grinned. "Just kidding. We won't."

33

"I did some cheerleading back home in Oklahoma." Chelsea jumped high, spun around in midair, and landed in a squat. "It might be fun to try here too." Then she shook her head. "But if I did that, I wouldn't have time for other things I want to do. Did you think about that, Kathy?"

"I guess not. It does take a lot of time." Kathy grinned. "But it's worth it to be on the team. I'd do anything to be on it!"

"Then let Mike show you some really fantastic moves." Chelsea started toward the stairs. "He'd probably show you some right now."

"Great!" Kathy followed Chelsea up the stairs with Roxie and Hannah close behind. They ran across the street to Chelsea's freshly mowed yard. Mike was doing front and back flips for two of his friends. He was only eight, but he was already almost a pro.

"Hey, Mike!" Chelsea called. "Kathy wants you to teach her some great moves."

Mike landed on his feet just a few inches away from Kathy. His blond hair and face were wet with sweat. He grinned, showing an empty space where a new tooth was poking through. "What do you want to learn?"

"I'm going to be a cheerleader, and I'd like to know how to do great cartwheels and flips."

"I'll show you. You have to put your hands down just right and hold your legs and feet just right." Mike did cartwheels from one side of the yard to the other, then did flips. He landed on his feet and flung his arms high as he arched his back.

Kathy clapped along with the others. If she could do as well as Mike, she'd be sure to make the team.

Mike ran to Kathy and showed her what he knew, and then she tried it. She could do a cartwheel, but not as cleanly as Mike. She tried time after time until she felt hot and tired. She dropped to the grass in the shade of a tree. "I'm too awkward, Mike."

"No, Kathy, you're too tense. Relax and do what I said."

"I can't."

Mike tugged Kathy's curl. "You come practice with me, and you'll be doing it as good as me."

Kathy sighed heavily. "I don't know when I'd have time to practice with you." Then she thought about the times she spent in the park with Megan. She asked Mike if he could join her there every morning, and he agreed. Smiling, Kathy pumped his hand up and down. "Thanks, Mike. See you in the morning."

"Sure." Mike looked at Kathy thoughtfully. "Will you do something for me?"

"Sure. Anything."

"See if Brody would teach me guitar."

Kathy's face fell. "I don't know, Mike. Why not ask him yourself?"

"Oh, I can't! He's too good."

"Then ask Duke to teach you."

"I did, but he won't. He said he's not a good teacher. And he said if I wanted Brody to teach me, I'd have to ask him myself." Mike hiked up his shorts. "But I just can't! Please, Kathy, ask Brody for me."

Kathy sighed heavily. "All right, I will. But he might not want to do it, you know."

"But he might. He just might! Ask him today, will you? And call me when you do."

Kathy nodded. She didn't want to talk to Brody about anything, but one favor deserved another.

A few minutes later Kathy pedaled home. She didn't want to think about talking to Brody, but she had to do it anyway. She'd promised Mike, and she never broke her word.

In the house she heard guitar music coming from Dad's music room. Slowly she walked toward it. The smell of Mom's perfume hung in the air.

Kathy slowly opened the door and stepped inside. Brody sat on a chair, his head bent over his guitar as he practiced. He was alone in the room. The keyboard and guitars stood near a wall. Sunlight streamed through the french doors onto the carpet. Kathy walked slowly toward the piano. Her legs felt rubbery. She wanted to run out without speaking to Brody!

"Brody," she said just above a whisper.

He lifted his head, then froze, his hands on the guitar. A red flush crept up his neck and over his face and ears. He ducked his head. "Did you . . . want to talk to me?"

Kathy nodded. "Mike McCrea wants to know if you'd teach him to play the guitar. He's Chelsea's little brother."

Brody glanced up at Kathy, then looked quickly away. "Why me?"

"He thinks you're really good."

"I guess I could."

"I'll tell him." Kathy waited for Brody to look up again, but he didn't. She rushed out of the room and closed the door with a firm click. Why was Brody so rude to her? She didn't deserve that kind of treatment.

Pressing her lips tightly together, Kathy ran to her bedroom and closed the door. She sank to the edge of her bed and rubbed her hand over her emerald-green and cream spread. As soon as she calmed down she'd call Mike. "I should tell him to stay as far away from Brody as he can get," she muttered.

Finally she jumped up and changed into her yellow T-shirt and blue shorts. She started to pin her *I'm A Best Friend* button on, then dropped it back on her desk. Alyssa would make fun of it.

Kathy walked to the empty kitchen and called the McCreas. Mike answered on the first ring. "Brody said he'd teach you."

"Yes!" Mike cried. "Thanks, Kathy. I'll be over as soon as I can."

"Go around to the back. Brody's in the music room." They talked a while longer, and then Kathy hung up. She found Mom in her office going over a student's file. She taught high school English during the year and tutored kids during the summer. She looked tired.

"I'm going to Alyssa's now, Mom."

"That's fine. Be nice, but don't let her boss you around like she used to do."

"She *is* the leader, Mom."

"I know. But a leader doesn't have to hurt the followers. If she gets too bossy, come back home. You can be a cheerleader without Alyssa."

Kathy bit back an argument. Mom didn't understand how it was. She wouldn't be accepted as a cheerleader if Alyssa didn't want her to be one. After all, her aunt was the one who decided who would be cheerleaders and who wouldn't. The other girls knew that as well as she did. "See you later, Mom."

"Bye, hon." Mom smiled. "You'll make a fine cheerleader, and don't you forget it! You have talent, and you've kept up your practice, so you'll do fine."

Kathy smiled and hurried away. Outdoors the

warm wind blew against her as she ran down the sidewalk and into Alyssa's shady yard. The others were already there, and Alyssa was telling them the first cheer they were going to practice. They all wore their yellow T-shirts and blue shorts.

"Hi," Kathy said.

"You're late!" Alyssa snapped.

Kathy glanced at her watch. It was a couple of minutes before 2. "You said to be here at 2."

"The others came five minutes ago."

"But we haven't started yet," Debbie said, smiling at Kathy.

"Tell me what to do." Kathy stepped into line beside Justine. Kathy smiled, but Justine turned away as if they were strangers. Kathy bit her lip. Didn't Justine want the others to know they'd met and talked in the park?

"We're going to do the Middle School Cheer first." Alyssa counted off, and they started together, calling out the words and doing the motions.

Kathy missed the last jump. "Sorry."

"Don't let it happen again!" Alyssa snapped.

Kathy managed to smile. "I won't." She wanted to tell Alyssa there was no reason to yell at her, but she didn't. She missed part of every cheer, but she thought she was doing just fine considering she hadn't practiced with a group in over a year.

Her hands on her hips, Alyssa stepped up to

Kathy. "You have to do better than you did today or you can't stay in the group."

"It's my first day, Alyssa. It's not fair to tell me that." Kathy turned to the others. "Is it, girls?"

Justine looked down at the ground without a word. Debbie and Sharon shrugged.

"Don't try to get them to feel sorry for you," Alyssa snapped. "Now let's try again."

Kathy clenched her teeth to hold back a sharp remark.

"Well?" Alyssa glared at Kathy. "Are you ready?"

Kathy barely nodded. Alyssa was trying to make her quit, but she wasn't going to. Nothing would make her quit! Nothing!

4

Family Time

Scowling, Kathy pushed a radish around in her glass salad bowl. It was hard to eat with Brody sitting across the kitchen table from her. He'd taken a shower before dinner and had changed into clean jeans and a white T-shirt. His dark hair was combed neatly. He wasn't eating much either. Kathy picked up a pickle. Even the smell of the hamburger on her plate next to the potato chips didn't make her hungry. And Dad's grilled hamburger inside a warm bun and covered with catsup, mayonnaise, tomato, pickle, lettuce, and two thin slices of mild cheese were the best in the world. Kathy felt like kicking something—or someone. Why couldn't Brody be with his own family where he belonged so she could enjoy one of her favorite meals?

Dad set down his tall glass of iced tea. The ice cubes clinked against the glass. "Brody, what's this about you teaching Mike McCrea guitar?"

His face red, Brody darted a look at Kathy, then nodded.

"What are you charging him?"

"Nothing. It's a favor."

Kathy blinked in surprise.

Dad smiled. "That's nice of you. Maybe you should get some paying students as well. It would be a nice way to earn money for yourself."

"I don't know . . ." Brody's voice faded away.

Duke swallowed the bite of hamburger in his mouth. Since Dad had had his long ponytail cut off, Duke looked just like him—tall, thin, blue eyes, and blond curls. He was the opposite of Brody, who had dark hair and eyes. "You could do it. You taught me a lot."

Brody smiled. "Thanks."

Megan looked at her fingers. "If I pull on them every day, will they grow faster?"

Everyone laughed. Kathy couldn't manage more than a smile.

"It won't help at all," Mom said, patting Megan's hand. "Your fingers will grow just as fast as you do. And look how much bigger you are now than you were last year! Remember the sundress I wanted you to wear this morning?"

Megan snickered into her hand. "It wouldn't fit. I'm four now and not three. It fit when I was three."

Kathy moved restlessly. She wanted to excuse

herself and go to her room, but she knew she couldn't. Dinner was family time, when they all talked about their day, told jokes, or had serious talks.

When Megan finally finished talking about being four, Duke told about mowing a lawn for an older couple who thought he was going to ruin their flower beds. Mom told about a boy she was helping to learn reading and comprehension. At times she hated tutoring, but at other times she enjoyed it. She liked working with the boy because he listened and learned quickly. Dad told about a famous guest singer who was going to be on the show and how much he was looking forward to meeting him.

"You're quiet tonight, Kathy," Mom said. "How'd cheerleading go?"

Kathy shrugged. "All right. I missed a few jumps . . . But I'll make them with a little more practice." If Brody hadn't been there, she would've gone into great detail about her day. She couldn't with him sitting with his head down and his face red. Did even her voice irritate him?

Megan slipped off her chair and jumped around. "I'm a cheerleader. Am I doing it right, Kathy?"

"Not quite."

"When I grow big like you, I want to be a cheerleader." Megan hugged Kathy's arm and then ran back to her chair. "A cheerleader and a guitar player . . . and a teacher too."

Kathy took a bite of her hamburger. It was almost cold and tasted greasy. She managed to eat some of it while the others talked and laughed.

After cleaning up the dinner dishes, Kathy reluctantly walked to the park with Megan chattering beside her, Brody and Duke in front of her, and Mom and Dad in back. The temperature had dropped enough to make walking comfortable. Mom liked to walk around the trail in the park if it wasn't too hot out. She said it was good exercise for all of them.

Megan tugged on Kathy's hand. "Why aren't you listening to me, Kathy?"

"Sorry. I was thinking about something else."

"Probably cheerleading, right?"

Kathy shrugged. She couldn't say she was wishing Brody wasn't there.

"Or were you thinking about your best friends?"

Kathy shrugged again.

"Natalie was my very best friend, but Brody is now."

Kathy frowned. Which was worse—a make-believe friend or Brody Vangaar?

"Brody told me a long story today. And it was good!"

Kathy couldn't imagine Brody taking time to tell Megan a story. Was she making this up?

Megan finally ran to Brody and Duke. She pushed between them and held their hands. Kathy breathed a sigh of relief. She'd had too much of Megan's chatter.

At the park Kathy lagged behind, while the family walked on ahead on the path between tall pines, oaks, and maples. Megan's laughter drifted back. The fragrance of pine covered all the other smells. Kathy kicked a twig off the woodchip-covered trail. It had been fun coming to the park before Brody came along. Now he was ruining everything. She looked toward the path that cut off to Betina Quinn's house. The Best Friends and Duke had helped clean her huge house, cut her gigantic lawn, and weed her beautiful flower gardens. She'd let everything go because she was so sad. The Best Friends and Megan had helped her trust Jesus to give her joy again. Kathy wished she could run to Betina's house and talk to her. Maybe she and Lee Malcomb had set their wedding date. Kathy sighed. She knew Mom and Dad wouldn't let her visit Betina during the family outing.

Kathy heard a movement behind her. She glanced back, then stopped short when she saw Justine Gold. She was wearing jeans, a short plaid blouse, and white sneakers. Kathy smiled. "Hi. I didn't know you were there."

Justine shrugged. "I decided to come for another walk."

"Want to walk with me?"

"I guess." Justine stepped up beside Kathy, and they walked slowly along the trail. Several people passed them, walking fast.

"Practice went okay today, don't you think?" Kathy asked.

"I don't know. Alyssa's mean sometimes."

"I know."

Justine was quiet a long time. "I shouldn't have told you about my folks arguing. Don't tell anybody, will you?"

Kathy's heart sank. What could she say? Finally she mumbled, "Okay."

"I was really upset. You've always been easy to talk to, so I told you. But I shouldn't have! Mom and Dad hate to have others know about our family problems."

"I'd help if I could."

"Thanks." Justine pushed her hands into the pockets of her jeans. "I did pray like you said."

"That's good."

Suddenly Justine stopped and pointed up ahead at Megan, Brody, and Duke. "Is that Brody Vangaar with your brother?"

Kathy frowned questioningly. "Yes."

Justine gasped. "But why?"

Kathy flushed painfully. "He lives with us now."

"I can't believe it!" Justine lowered her voice. "Do you know his brother's in jail for dealing drugs?"

"I know."

"What if Brody does drugs?"

"He doesn't."

"Maybe he does and you just don't know about it. I can't believe you actually have him living in your house! Alyssa's going to really be angry when she hears about it."

Kathy frowned. "Why should *she* care?"

"She only lives two houses away from you! And she hates Brody and his brother. Cole Vangaar sold drugs to her cousin, and he died!"

Kathy pressed her hand to her throat. "That's terrible!"

"Really terrible!"

Kathy watched two girls run past, then spoke when they were out of hearing. "But Brody's not Cole."

"Same family." Justine flipped her long dark blonde hair back. "I know I'd be afraid to have him live in *my* house."

Her head spinning, Kathy walked slowly along, and Justine finally joined her. Brody, Duke, and Megan disappeared around a bend in the trail. "I can't do anything about him living with us. Dad has legal custody of him."

"I can't believe it!"

Kathy didn't want to talk about Brody a second longer. "Do you think we'll make it on the team at tryouts?"

"Sure. We're all good."

"What if Alyssa tells her aunt we're not?"

Justine hunched her shoulders. "I wish Alyssa's aunt wasn't the one in charge of the team, although Debbie says Alyssa's aunt will judge fairly."

"She didn't last year. She took Alyssa's word about Sari Roschild. And you know Sari was good!"

"Alyssa *said* her aunt took her word about Sari. Who knows if it's really true. Maybe Sari crumbled under the pressure of tryouts."

"She and Alyssa still aren't talking to each other."

"I know." Justine shook her head. "I don't like the way Alyssa is, but she's good at cheerleading, and her aunt knows that. Whoever works with Alyssa is sure to have a better chance of being on the team."

"Then I won't let her make me get mad and quit."

Just then Justine stopped and pointed ahead. "Look! Brody and Duke are coming back. I'm leaving." She spun around and ran back the way she'd come.

Kathy almost followed her, then decided to keep going. Would Alyssa make it impossible for her to make the team? Kathy pressed her lips tightly together. "She'd better not!" Kathy walked faster, her head down, her mind on Alyssa.

"You're a slowpoke, Kathy," Duke said, laughing.

Kathy glanced up and scowled. Brody and Duke stood in her path. Duke was smiling, and Brody was looking down with his face red. Kathy knotted her fists. "So?"

Duke's smile vanished. "Hey, I was only teasing."

Kathy frowned at Brody, then ran toward Mom and Dad and Megan. She wouldn't talk to Duke with Brody standing there with his face red and his head down. Recently she and Duke had finally become friends, and now Brody was even ruining that!

An hour later Kathy sat at the kitchen table with a hot fudge sundae. Her family laughed and talked as they ate. But Brody was silent. Kathy took a bite. The vanilla ice cream was cold and delicious, the hot fudge soft and gooey. This was usually one of her favorite times of the day, but Brody ruined it all just by being there. It wasn't fair! She forced the rest of her sundae down just to keep the family from asking her if something was wrong. They all knew she loved hot fudge sundaes.

Dad finished his sundae and pushed his glass bowl forward, then leaned his elbows on the table. "Brody, I heard from my friend at the Police Department that Cole might be turned loose because of lack of space in the jail."

Brody gulped. "He can't come get me and make me go with him, can he?"

"No. I have legal custody." Dad looked serious. "But Cole might try to visit you, even though he's not allowed to."

"I know." Brody trembled. "He's always done what he wanted when he wanted."

"If you see him, tell us." Mom looked around the table. "If any of you see him, tell us. We don't want him to cause trouble for Brody or for us."

Kathy locked her hands in her lap as Megan asked all kinds of questions about Cole Vangaar. Kathy remembered when Cole had tried to hurt Duke for helping Brody. She didn't want that to happen again. Maybe it would be better for all of them if Brody were sent somewhere else to live—like in Grand Rapids or even in Detroit, clear across the state.

Mom finally changed the subject and asked, "Where shall we have our picnic Sunday? At the park in town, or maybe at the park at the zoo?"

"The zoo!" Megan cried, jumping up and down.

"The zoo." Dad nodded and smiled. "Boys? Kathy?"

"The zoo," Duke said, and Brody barely nodded.

Kathy shrugged. She didn't care. With Brody coming on the picnic with them, it would be ruined anyway.

"Then it's the zoo." Mom brushed a strand of hair off her round cheek. "We'll go right after church, eat in the park there, then walk through the zoo. It sounds like a great plan to me." She laughed.

Megan ran to Mom and hugged her tightly. "I want to go to the petting zoo and pet all the baby animals." She turned to Kathy. "Want to pet the baby animals with me?"

"No!" Kathy wanted to grab back the harsh word, but it was too late. She watched Megan pucker up her face. "Sorry, Megan. Sure, I'll pet the babies with you."

"I knew you would." Megan hugged Kathy, then ran to Dad and asked him the same question.

Mom looked questioningly at Kathy but didn't say anything. Kathy was glad.

Later in her bedroom Kathy slowly changed into her blue summer pajamas. A cool breeze blew in her open window and fluttered her curtains. The smell of the flowers outside her window drifted in.

"Kathy . . ." Mom knocked and poked her head through the doorway. "Can we come in?"

"Sure." Kathy sank to her chair and watched Mom and Dad walk in. They still wore their shorts, shirts, and walking shoes.

"Kit Kat, what's bothering you?" Dad rested his hand lightly on Kathy's blonde curls.

"We know *something* is." Mom leaned against the desk and studied Kathy.

"It's Brody. I don't want him to live with us."

"Oh my . . ." Mom bit her lip and looked up at Dad.

Dad sighed heavily. "Kathleen, Kathleen . . . I don't know what to say. We can't send Brody away. I thought you'd agreed to have him come here."

"I didn't know he hated me so much."

"Kathy!" Mom stood straighter and stared at Kathy in surprise. "He doesn't hate you. What gave you such an idea?"

"The way he acts around me."

"He's shy with you," Dad said. "But he'll get over that. Be patient with him. He's never had a sister before."

"He gets along fine with Megan." Kathy jumped up. "I *know* he doesn't like me. I don't want him here!"

Dad slipped his arms around Kathy and held her close. "I'm sorry you feel that way. We'll pray that you'll change your mind."

Kathy smelled Dad's aftershave and the slight smell of sweat. She leaned against him for a moment, then pulled away. "He's not part of our family, Dad. Why do we have to have him here?"

"We want to help him." Dad kissed Kathy's cheek. "You'll feel differently when you get to know each other better and he stops being shy around you."

Kathy wanted to disagree, but she kept the words locked inside her.

Mom hugged Kathy and kissed her cheek. "God's Word says His love is shed abroad in your heart by the Holy Spirit. He'll help you love Brody the way you should." Mom kissed Kathy again. "I love you. Sleep tight."

Kathy managed to smile. "Good night." She stood in the middle of her room as they walked out and closed the door. She thought about the Scripture Mom had quoted. The Best Friends had read the very same verse not long ago. Kathy frowned. She wouldn't think about it right now. Brody didn't like her, and she wasn't going to like him—that's all there was to it.

With a heavy sigh Kathy walked slowly to the bathroom to brush her teeth.

5

Alyssa's Threat

In front of the Logan house, Kathy lugged the last black garbage bag to the street and piled it on the mound of plastic bags. She wiped sweat from her forehead and pressed her hand to her back. She'd already gone to the park with Megan this morning and had practiced doing flips and cartwheels with Mike. He was a good teacher. By the end of the hour she was doing much better cartwheels, though she had bruises from falling a few times.

Glancing at the two-story frame house in front of her, Kathy listened to the laughter drifting out of the outside door leading to the basement. She and the Best Friends had agreed to clean the basement for Turner Logan. His mother-in-law was coming to live with him and his wife, and Turner was making an apartment for her in the basement. Roxie's dad knew the Logans, so they knew it was safe to work for them. The *King's Kids* had agreed ahead of time that they wouldn't work for anyone until one of the parents checked the person out. So far they'd had to turn down only three jobs.

"I wish we'd turned this job down," she muttered as she walked back down the stairs. She didn't have time for a job. Her mind was full of how to get rid of Brody and how to keep Alyssa happy.

Her hands dirty and a cobweb in her red hair, Chelsea held a broom out to Kathy. "You can sweep that wall down."

"What if I don't want to?"

Chelsea gasped. "Kathy! That's not like you at all. Is something wrong?"

Kathy flushed and took the broom. It *wasn't* like her to answer in a sharp manner.

Chelsea turned to Roxie and Hannah. "Girls, come here quick. Something's wrong with Kathy."

Concerned, Hannah ran to Kathy and looked her over. "Did you hurt yourself? Can I get you a drink of water?"

"You look fine to me," Roxie said. "Are you trying to get out of work?"

"Roxie!" Chelsea shook her finger at Roxie. "Don't make her feel worse than she does." Chelsea turned back to Kathy. "What's wrong, honey?"

Kathy grinned. Chelsea was trying hard to stop calling people "honey" the way they did in Oklahoma. Michigan folks felt strange being called "honey" by someone outside their own families.

"I'm all right, Chel. It's Brody. It's really hard having him live with us. I mean it."

"You'll probably get used to it," Hannah said. "It took me a while to get used to my baby brother." She giggled. "It took me a while to get used to the twins and my other sister too."

"This is different." Kathy leaned against a steel support post. Cobwebs hung from the ceiling and dangled from corner to corner of the concrete blocks. "Brody wasn't born into our family."

"Mike sure likes him," Chelsea said. "Mike doesn't even have a guitar, but Brody said he could practice on his until he got one."

Kathy frowned. She didn't want to hear anything nice about Brody. "Dad said Cole Vangaar might be getting out of jail soon. That would put us in danger."

Roxie shivered. "That's scary."

"We have angels watching over us," Hannah said softly.

Chelsea stepped closer to Kathy and motioned for Hannah and Roxie to move closer too. "Back in Oklahoma there was a woman who saw an angel. Actually saw one! She said three men jumped out at her late at night when she was walking to her car. She said to them, 'You leave me alone in the name of Jesus!' Suddenly a big angel stood beside her. The men ran away fast. The angel walked the woman to her car, then disappeared. So she got home safely."

Roxie frowned. "Is that true?"

"Yes!" Chelsea nodded firmly. "The Bible says God sends angels to guard us all the time."

"Do you ever have trouble believing stories like that?" Roxie plucked nervously at her blouse. "I do. And sometimes I wonder if the miracles Jesus did were really real."

"I believe what the Bible says because it's God's Word," Hannah said gently. "And I believe there are angels because the Bible says so."

"I believe so too." Kathy nodded. She couldn't understand how Roxie could question it. Then she remembered Roxie hadn't gone to church or read her Bible as much as the rest of them. She'd accepted Jesus as her Savior, but her family hadn't until just a few months ago. Now they prayed and had Bible reading together as a family. Just then Kathy remembered the verse Mom had quoted about God's love being in her heart and how because of it she could love Brody. Impatiently Kathy pushed the thought aside. It made her feel guilty. "We aren't going to finish this job if we don't get to work!"

"See—she snapped again!" Chelsea waved her hand. "I told you something was wrong with Kathy!" Chelsea pushed her face right up to Kathy's. "What is it?"

Kathy frowned. Chelsea's face looked like one big blur of freckles. "I told you—it's Brody!"

57

"There's more though." Chelsea nodded. "I can tell."

Kathy couldn't tell them the whole truth—or could she? "Oh, okay! It's cheerleading too. Alyssa Carroll's not very nice to me."

"She's *never* been nice to me," Hannah said, wrinkling her nose.

"Oh, I remember her!" Roxie nodded so hard her short cap of dark hair bounced. "She tripped me in science class last year! I was sooo embarrassed!"

"Have I met her?" Chelsea asked.

"Probably not," Kathy said. "She doesn't go to our church. But you'll meet her when school starts."

Chelsea sighed heavily. "I won't like going to a new school!"

Just then Hannah looked at her watch. "Oh no! I have to be home in half an hour! And we're not even done here!" She grabbed a broom and started sweeping down cobwebs.

Kathy took her broom and carefully swept the ceiling and wall in her area. She sneezed from the dust, then sneezed again. A cobweb fell in her hair. Shivering, she brushed it away. She was going to have to take a shower before she went to cheerleading practice. Her stomach knotted. Could she face Alyssa again today? Yes! She had to or she wouldn't have a chance to be on the team.

Across the room Roxie said, "How's Justine? Is she still worried about her parents?"

Kathy stiffened. Slowly she turned to Roxie. "I told Justine I wouldn't talk about it."

"Oh, is it that bad?" Roxie clicked her tongue. "That's a shame. I asked Mom if she knew the Golds were having trouble."

Kathy bit back a groan. What if Justine learned she'd told the Best Friends? "Please don't talk about them anymore. It'll make Justine feel bad."

Roxie shrugged. "Okay."

Her mind whirling with thoughts of Justine, Kathy finished her share of the work. She stood the broom in the corner and brushed her hands together. "I have to go now. See you later."

"Can we watch you practice today?" Chelsea asked.

Kathy shook her head. "Not yet. I wasn't that good yesterday. But I'll do better today."

"Don't forget about our sleepover tonight at Chelsea's," Roxie said.

"I won't." Kathy smiled. She liked Chelsea's fabulous rec room. Her dad had had it built as a surprise for the family when they'd moved in. It had a big-screen TV, games of all kinds, and a snack bar. "I'll bring chips and cheese for nachos."

"That makes me hungry right now." Chelsea giggled. "I rented a video you'll love! It's a comedy, but that's all I'll tell you."

"I can't wait!" Hannah tipped her head back and laughed. "Sleepovers are sooo much fun!"

"But we don't get much sleep," Roxie said with a grin. "I wonder why it's called a *sleep*over."

"See you all tonight." Kathy waved, then ran to her bike. The sun burned down on her. Finally she reached the row of shade trees. A dog barked behind a white picket fence. A pickup drove past, music blaring out the open window. The smell of exhaust fumes filled the air and then were gone.

At home Kathy took a quick shower, glad for the rush of cool water over her hot skin. In her room she dressed in her yellow T-shirt and blue shorts. She tied her sneakers, then ran to the kitchen for lunch. Megan was already there with Duke and Brody. Mom and Dad were both at work. The kitchen smelled like grilled cheese sandwiches.

Smiling excitedly, Megan held up her sandwich. "Look, Kathy! Brody made it for me. I got hungry. Duke was busy, and you weren't here. Isn't Brody nice?"

"I guess." Kathy darted a glance at Brody. He met her gaze, then looked quickly away with a crimson flush. She wanted to yell at him. Why wasn't he nice to her? Then it wouldn't be so bad having him here.

"Mom called and said she'd be late," Duke said as he set his glass of punch down. "You'll have to watch Megan."

Kathy gasped. "No! I have cheerleading practice! You know that, Duke."

"But I have to mow the Driscolls' lawn."

"I can watch myself," Megan said in a small voice. "Natalie will be with me. Won't you, Natalie?"

Kathy's heart sank. Natalie again! "Maybe you could mow the lawn later, Duke."

"I can't. I already called to ask."

Brody cleared his throat. "I'll watch Megan. Is that all right with you, Megan?"

"Sure! Thanks, Brody." Megan hugged him tightly around the neck. "I didn't want to stay with Natalie anyway."

Kathy stared at Brody in surprise. "Will you really watch her?"

Brody barely nodded. He looked down at his plate.

"Thanks."

Without looking up Brody said, "I like watching her."

Kathy could tell he meant it. No wonder Megan loved him. Kathy opened the cheese and sliced off several pieces. Why couldn't Brody be nice to *her*? She pushed the thought aside and quickly made a sandwich and filled a glass with punch. She ate without speaking. She listened to Megan talk to Brody and Duke. Duke didn't say much, but Brody actually answered all of Megan's questions. He did it without hesitation and without turning red. Kathy excused herself and hurried out of the kitchen, her heart hammering against her rib cage. Why was Brody so nice to Megan and so mean to her?

"Who even cares?" Kathy muttered as she walked to her bedroom to relax a while before going to practice. This time she planned to get there five minutes early. She didn't want to give Alyssa any reason to snap at her.

Five minutes before 2 Kathy stepped into Alyssa's yard. No one was there. The trees shaded the rich green grass. A slight breeze blew against the bright flowers. Kathy's heart sank. Had they decided to practice somewhere else and not tell her?

Slowly Kathy walked toward the house. Before she reached the door Justine, Debbie, and Sharon ran into the yard. Kathy breathed a sigh of relief as she joined them.

Sharon looked around. "Where's Alyssa?"

Kathy shrugged. "I just got here."

Justine frowned at the house. "She's probably inside waiting for two o'clock. Then she'll come out and yell at us for being here so early."

"I wish her aunt wasn't the leader and judge of the team," Debbie said.

Kathy moved restlessly. "We could talk to the middle school principal and tell him what's going on."

"Oh, wow!" Sharon shook her head. "I don't know about that."

"Leave things the way they are," Justine snapped. "It's always better that way."

Kathy wondered if Justine was talking more about her parents than about the cheerleading dilemma.

The door burst open, and Alyssa ran out. Her hair was neatly brushed and held back by a wide yellow band over the top of her head. She stopped right in front of Kathy. "So Brody Vangaar lives at your house!"

Kathy darted a look at Justine. She looked guilty, so Kathy knew she'd told Alyssa.

"I don't want Brody to live on the same street as me," Alyssa snapped. "His brother killed my cousin!"

"But Brody didn't," Kathy said weakly.

"They're the same to me!" Alyssa lifted her chin, and sparks flew from her blue eyes. "Tell him to leave."

"But I can't! It's up to my folks."

Alyssa knotted her fists. "If you don't find a way to make him leave, you can't practice with us, and then you won't have a chance to be on the team."

Kathy cried out as if she'd been struck. She heard the other girls gasp.

"I'll give you three days." Alyssa whipped around to face the others. "Let's practice now."

Kathy turned toward the sidewalk. She felt she should leave right then, but she couldn't. Her shoulders slumped, she stepped into line beside Justine.

6

The Sleepover

Her stomach a tight, hard ball, Kathy sat on the wooden stool at the high counter and watched Chelsea stick the plate of nachos in the microwave. Roxie and Hannah were playing a game of Ping-Pong. Kathy heard the ball bounce back and forth. She should've stayed home tonight. But if she had, the Best Friends would've come looking for her. Then she would've broken down and told them what Alyssa had said about getting rid of Brody or leaving the practice team. Kathy knew what the Best Friends would've said. They'd think she was terrible for staying when Alyssa had made such an outrageous demand. Somebody needed to stand up to Alyssa. Kathy bit her lip. It wasn't going to be her!

"Here are the nachos." Chelsea set the plate on the counter in front of Kathy. "Girls, the nachos are ready."

"Ummm . . . They smell great." Roxie ran to

the counter and hoisted herself onto the tall stool. She wore jeans and a green pullover. She picked up a chip covered with melted cheese and pushed it into her mouth. "It's great," she said around the chip and cheese.

Hannah took one and ate it in two bites. She reached for another, then stopped. "What's wrong, Kathy? How come you're not eating your nachos? They're your very favorite!"

"I guess I'm just not hungry."

"What?" Chelsea shrieked, clamping her hand to Kathy's forehead. "She's sick for sure!"

Kathy pulled away and dropped off the stool. "Cut it out, Chelsea." The Best Friends stared in shock at Kathy. She flushed. "What?"

"Okay, Kathleen Aber. Tell us what's wrong." Hannah crossed her arms and looked sternly at Kathy.

"Tell us right now!" Chelsea stood shoulder to shoulder with Hannah.

Roxie joined them. "Start talking."

Kathy's lip quivered. She would not cry! Tears stung her eyes, and she blinked them away.

"Don't leave anything out!"

Kathy shook her head, then decided she had to tell or she'd be unhappy forever. With a catch in her voice she told them what Alyssa had said to her.

"I can't believe it!" Roxie screwed up her face

and doubled her fists. "What can we do to her? Give me time and I'll think of something!"

Hannah shook her head. "We can't get even. You know that, Roxie. Jesus said not to."

Roxie grinned sheepishly. "I forgot again. Sorry."

"We'll pray for Alyssa." Chelsea crossed her arms and looked thoughtful. "I think we should talk to her aunt. Why would her aunt let Alyssa do that to the girls? It's not right."

"And we'll find a way to convince Alyssa that Brody won't cause trouble for anyone and that he's not like his brother." Hannah wagged her finger. "If she knew him, she'd know that."

Kathy licked her dry lips. This was going to be hard to say, but she'd say it anyway. "I can't convince Alyssa of anything about Brody. I want him out of the house! I don't like him at all!" There— she'd said it! She waited for the girls to scold her, but they didn't. She breathed a sigh of relief. She couldn't take a scolding tonight or she'd burst into tears and never stop crying.

"Kathy, you already know the answer," Hannah said softly. "You're the one who helps us do what Jesus wants."

"I know . . . But not this time." Kathy took a deep shuddering breath. "You see, I don't want to love Brody, no matter what Jesus says."

"Oh, Kathy . . ." Chelsea caught Kathy's hand

and held it tightly. "That's rebellion against God. You don't want to do that."

Roxie gasped. "Rebellion against God! How can you say that to her, Chel? That's terrible."

Her face serious, Chelsea turned to Roxie. "It's true. If you refuse to follow what God says in His Word, that's rebellion against Him. Isn't that right, Hannah?"

"Yes."

Kathy's eyes filled with tears. "You're right, and I know it too, but I didn't want to think about it."

"Now that you have, you want to obey, don't you?"

Kathy slowly nodded. Chelsea was right. She did want to obey. That's really why she'd finally told them what she was thinking and feeling.

"Let's pray together." Hannah reached for Kathy's and Roxie's hands. They all stood in the circle, and Hannah prayed that Kathy would do what God wanted her to do—love Brody, forgive Alyssa, and do what she could to keep Alyssa from hurting Brody.

While Chelsea prayed for the right words to say to Alyssa's aunt, Kathy silently asked God to forgive her. A great peace settled over her, and she smiled. She was glad the Best Friends prayed together. That made their friendship even stronger.

A few minutes later Chelsea led them to the

thick multicolored cushions on the floor. When they were seated she said, "Now, how can we help Kathy and Brody become friends?"

Kathy covered her face and groaned. "Friends? Do we have to go that far?"

Chelsea nodded. "Remember when you and Duke became friends? You were thankful for it. Rob and I have always been friends. Brothers and sisters don't have to fight all the time—they can have fun together. You and Brody can be friends . . . Really."

"We have rules on making friends." Roxie held up her hand to count them off on her fingers as she went. "Ask Brody about himself—his likes and dislikes. Be friendly to him. Make him feel at ease around you. Give him a rose." Roxie giggled. The Best Friends had left a rosebud on her doorstep to let her know they loved her—and to tease her. "If he is shy like Hannah said, talk him out of his shyness. If you're right and he doesn't like you, show him what a nice person you are. We'll tell him how nice you are too."

Kathy laughed. "I can see it now—you three lined up in a row to tell Brody how wonderful I am. I don't think he'd listen."

"You never can tell. We can be really persuasive." Roxie giggled and nudged Chelsea. "Right?"

"Sure can!" Chelsea laughed, then grew serious. "I had a dream last night." She bit her lip.

Kathy leaned forward in anticipation.

"I dreamed nobody liked me. Nobody at all! It was really really awful. I woke up crying."

Hannah patted Chelsea's arm. "But you know it's not true. We all like you."

"We do!" Kathy added.

Roxie rubbed her *I'm A Best Friend* button. "I sometimes have that same dream."

Hannah brushed a tear off her dark lash. "Before I got to know you girls, I never had a friend. Not one! I had my family and all my relatives, but that's different. It's awful not having a friend. I'm really thankful I have you three. I mean it!"

Kathy nodded. "I had friends before, but not friends who prayed *with* me and prayed *for* me. And not friends I could tell secrets to. Some people don't keep secrets." Kathy thought about Justine and flushed painfully. "Justine told me about her parents, and I told you girls. I shouldn't have, and I'm really sorry. I don't know how to tell Justine I told. It makes it hard to be with her."

"It would be hard to tell her, that's for sure," Roxie said.

"I had to tell two girls who once were my friends back in Oklahoma that I wouldn't watch an R-rated video with them. They said nobody would ever know. I said I wouldn't watch it because it's wrong to pollute our minds like that. They laughed at me and never talked to me again."

"I'm afraid that's what Justine will do." Kathy

wrapped her arms around her legs and rested her chin on her knees. "I like Justine . . . Not as a very best friend like you girls, but I'd like to be friends with her." Kathy looked at the Best Friends. "I think it's good to have other friends too, don't you? We don't want to keep everybody out of our lives like some girls I know."

Chelsea nodded. "Sometimes girls get into groups and get angry when another girl tries to join in. I hope it's not that way at school. Is it?"

"Yes," Hannah said.

"No," Kathy said. They all laughed. "I guess it's both ways, depending on the girls." Kathy tapped her chest. "I would never push anyone away if they wanted to be friends."

"Me neither." Roxie jumped up. "That's enough talk for now! I'm ready for a game. How about Clue? Anyone want to solve a mystery?"

Kathy hurried to the table where Clue was already set up. "I'll be Miss Scarlet."

The others called off who they wanted to be, and the game began. About an hour later Hannah won. Then they played another, and Kathy won.

"Who wants chocolate-chip cookies and ice cream?" Chelsea ran to the refrigerator and pulled out the ice cream. The chocolate-chip cookies sat on the counter in a plastic bag.

"Wouldn't it be fun to work in an ice cream store and be able to eat any flavor you wanted whenever you wanted?" Roxie dipped her spoon into the ice cream and ate the bite with her eyes closed. "Ummmm good."

"I'd like to work in a department store like your sister Lacy does, Roxie," Chelsea said as she broke a cookie into her ice cream. "Then I could get clothes at a discount. I'd buy jeans and dresses. And sweaters! I saw a blue and green and black sweater that was absolutely gorgeous a few days ago! But it cost way too much for me."

Hannah leaned on her hand with her chin. "I think I'd like to be a teacher like your mom, Kathy. I'd teach kids that we are all equal, no matter what color our skin is."

"I would never be a teacher! Mom says some of the kids talk back to her. And some of them never do their work." Kathy took a bite of ice cream and let it slide down her throat. "Of course, she has some smart kids and kids who like to learn too. But I still wouldn't want to be a teacher. Well, unless I taught gym class and cheerleading. That would be fun."

"Then you'd be the person who'd have to see that the girls took showers after gym. And you know how hard that is." Roxie laughed. "You hated taking showers last year, Kathy."

"That's because we had to shower right out in the open where all the girls could see. You think I want everybody looking at me while I take a shower? If I were the teacher, I'd make the school get showers with curtains or doors."

"I'd make the school get food you can eat." Roxie wrinkled her nose. "Do you know how terrible most of the food tastes?"

"I have it!" Chelsea jumped up and down and laughed. "We'll start a new business! We'll make real food and sell it to the schools! We'd make a fortune! Who wouldn't want real food instead of imitation food from a can or a box?"

"This is even better!" Kathy's eyes twinkled. "We could invent a can and a box to be eaten with the food inside it! We wouldn't have to recycle the cans or boxes. The cook would melt them in the food and we'd eat them! Nobody would know the difference." Kathy giggled at her ridiculous idea.

The others groaned. Chelsea ran to the TV and picked up a video. "I think it's time to watch the video. You're funny, Kathy, but this is funnier."

"Maybe I'll be a comedienne when I grow up." Kathy ran to her cushion and flopped down on it.

"What's the video?" Hannah asked as Chelsea pushed it into the VCR.

"It's a Christian comedy." Chelsea pushed Play, then ran to her cushion with the remote in her hand. "My aunt saw it and said she laughed so hard she rolled on the floor. She thought we'd like it."

Kathy flopped on her stomach with her chin in her hands and watched as the movie began. She laughed along with the others. The movie ended too soon. "Let's watch it again."

"Yeah, let's," Hannah said.

Chelsea rewound it and started it over. "Wouldn't it be fun to be an actress?"

"And make lots of money," Hannah said.

"We'd be celebrities!" Chelsea sashayed across the basement floor in a model's pose.

Laughing, Kathy jumped up and joined her. "Like this . . ." She exaggerated the walk Chelsea was doing. The girls laughed.

"The movie started!" Hannah sat cross-legged and stared at the big screen.

Kathy grabbed a bag of chocolate candy, took a handful, and passed it on to Roxie.

Much later Kathy pulled a pink comforter up over her and sleepily closed her eyes. The room was finally quiet around her. She smiled. Having a sleepover was the best thing in the world—especially with her own best friends. She yawned and snuggled deep into her pillow. Right now she felt like she could convince Brody to be friends. Tomorrow she'd talk to him. Maybe he didn't hate her after all. She'd even talk to Alyssa and convince her Brody was all right.

Kathy smiled and drifted off to sleep.

7

The Note

Kathy yawned as she walked slowly into her house. The only bad thing about having a sleepover was staying awake the next day. It was almost noon, but it felt like 6 in the morning. The house sounded empty. Smells of coffee and french toast drifted through the kitchen.

"Mom? Dad? Anybody home?" Kathy listened for an answer, but none came. Mom was probably shopping with Megan. Dad was usually home on Saturday mornings though. She ran to the music room, but it was empty, so she hurried to the study. Maybe Dad was there and hadn't heard her. The room was empty. Sunlight streamed through the windows onto the blue carpet. A folded paper on Dad's otherwise clean desk awakened her curiosity. She walked to the big desk and picked it up. It was lined paper torn from a spiral binder and folded in fourths. A shiver ran down her spine as she opened it. She read: "Brody Vangaar does drugs. I know he does. Don't let him stay. Send him away or else."

Kathy gasped. Or else what? Where had the note come from? It was printed in pencil by hand in unsteady letters. Could Alyssa have done it?

"Kathy?"

She jumped at Dad's voice and quickly stuck the note behind her back.

"What've you got there, Kathy?" Looking very stern, Dad slowly walked toward her.

She swallowed hard. She didn't want Dad to read the note. He'd know Brody really wasn't doing drugs, but still . . . Who would've written the note and put it on the desk?

Dad slowly held out his hand. "Give it here." His voice was gruff, not at all like his usual kind manner.

Her heart sank as she reluctantly laid the folded note in his hand.

He didn't even read the note but tapped it against his palm. "Kathy, I'm deeply disappointed that you would do this just to get rid of Brody."

"Dad!" Her voice came out in a weak croak. He thought she'd written it!

"I found it yesterday on the piano in my music room. I know you planned for Brody to see it so he'd leave without a word. I asked him about it, and he hadn't seen it. I didn't tell him what it said."

Kathy licked her dry lips. She tried to get words

past her dry throat. She knew Dad could think she'd done it because of the way she'd been acting and from what she'd said to him. But she hadn't written it!

"I am very disappointed in you." Dad looked ready to cry. "You've never done anything like this before. Is it really that hard to have Brody here?"

"Oh, Daddy . . ." Kathy burst into tears.

Dad pulled Kathy into his arms and held her.

Finally Kathy looked up at Dad. She smelled coffee on his breath. "I didn't write the note," she whispered hoarsely. "Honest, Daddy."

He looked deep into her eyes. "I can see you're telling the truth. I'm sorry for assuming you were guilty before I even talked to you. Forgive me?"

Kathy nodded. "And forgive me for wanting to get rid of Brody. I was wrong."

Dad hugged Kathy close again. "I'm glad you finally saw the truth."

"Me too."

Dad frowned. "Since you didn't write this, who did?" Dad slapped the note against his hand again. "Duke certainly wouldn't. Megan couldn't."

Kathy thought of Alyssa. "Did Brody or Duke leave your music room door unlocked—could somebody have slipped in?"

"I thought of that. I checked it myself, and it was locked."

"Then how did it get here? In the mail maybe?"

"I thought of that too." Dad dropped the note back on his desk. "But your mom got the mail, and she said there were only three bills."

"It's a mystery for sure." Kathy leaned weakly against Dad's desk. She hesitantly told Dad what Alyssa had said about making Brody leave. "She might've written the note."

"But how would she get it into my study?"

"Did she come over while Duke or Brody was in the study and leave it?"

"No. I asked them if anyone had come."

"Who else was here?"

Dad wrinkled his brow in thought. "Mike McCrea. But he would never write such a note. Brody is practically his hero."

"You're right."

Dad pushed his hands into the pocket of his faded jeans. "I'll have a talk with Alyssa's parents so they know Brody isn't on drugs and isn't anything like his brother Cole."

"Dad . . ." Kathy took a deep breath.

Dad cocked his brow. "Yes?"

"Could you wait a while before you talk to Alyssa's folks? Let me talk to Alyssa first. Please?"

Dad frowned thoughtfully. "Well, okay, I'll wait. Let me know how it comes out with Alyssa . . . And don't let her walk all over you."

Kathy squared her shoulders. "I won't!" She

started for the door, then turned back. "Is Brody home?"

Dad shook his head. "He and Duke are mowing lawns this morning. They'll be back sometime this afternoon. Why?"

Kathy shrugged. "I just wondered." She didn't want to tell Dad she was going to try to make friends with Brody just in case she backed out. She'd tell him after it happened. "I'm going to see Alyssa now. I'll be back later."

Dad nodded. "Remember what I said. Don't let her treat you badly."

"I won't." Kathy hurried to the kitchen, picked up her bag from the sleepover, and took it to her bedroom. She looked longingly at the bed. She'd like to sleep instead of talking to Alyssa. Kathy changed into green shorts and a T-shirt with bold green, yellow, and orange stripes across the front. She pulled on green socks and tied her white sneakers. She glanced in the mirror as she used an orange pick to fluff out her blonde curls. How would it feel to be able to use a regular comb and easily comb through her hair? Maybe she should have her hair cut as short as Roxie's and make it even easier to comb through. Kathy made a face, and the mirror reflected it right back at her. She giggled and ran from the bedroom.

Outdoors she squinted against the hot August sun. Soon it would be September and time for school to start. How would Brody be treated at school? Probably everyone knew his brother was in jail. That had to be embarrassing. Kathy frowned thoughtfully. She'd never thought about Cole being an embarrassment to Brody. She'd ask him about that. It wasn't Brody's fault that Cole had sold drugs and was in jail.

Kathy walked slowly down the sidewalk. Kids shouted and laughed in a backyard swimming pool across the street. She'd rather be swimming and having fun than face Alyssa. Kathy giggled under her breath. Actually she'd rather take a shower in gym than face Alyssa.

"But I'm going to do it anyway!" The words rang out, and Kathy laughed at her boldness.

Slowly Kathy walked up the shaded sidewalk to Alyssa's red front door. The house was a two-story gray frame house with red shutters and red doors. A pot of red geraniums stood on the middle step leading to the door. She heard the TV and someone laughing. Taking a deep breath, she rang the doorbell. Butterflies fluttered in her stomach, and she wanted to run back home as fast as she could. Silently she prayed for help, mostly for courage to face Alyssa.

The door opened, and Mr. Carroll stood there in jeans and a plaid shirt. "Hi, Kathy. Can I help you?"

"I'd like to talk to Alyssa."

"She's not home right now. I'll tell her you stopped by."

"Thanks." Kathy started to turn away.

"She tells me Brody Vangaar is staying at your place."

Kathy nodded. "But he's not like his brother. Honest! He's nice and not into drugs at all."

"I'm glad to hear that. I hope he doesn't make trouble for any of us."

"He won't . . . Really."

Mr. Carroll nodded without smiling. "I mean to talk to your dad about him."

"He's home now."

"Well, I don't need to right now." Mr. Carroll rubbed a hand over his thick brown hair. "But if Brody steps out of line, I'll have a whole lot to say. I don't want my kids exposed to drugs."

"Brody doesn't do drugs or sell them," Kathy said stiffly.

"Fine. I hope it stays that way." Mr. Carroll closed the door with a firm click.

Slowly Kathy walked down the sidewalk. Did the other neighbors think the same thing about Brody?

"Hey you . . . A Teddy Bear!"

Kathy's heart sank at Alyssa's nickname for her. She looked down the sidewalk as Alyssa ran toward her. Alyssa wore a short denim skirt and a white blouse. Her long hair was loose around her shoulders and bounced as she ran.

Her cheeks red, Alyssa stopped in front of Kathy. "We don't practice on Saturdays, and it's not even two o'clock! So why are you at my house?"

Kathy almost turned and ran, but she squared her shoulders and stood her ground. "I want you to know Brody is staying with us, and I won't do anything to make him leave. And I'm going to keep practicing cheerleading."

"Not with us you're not!"

"The girls already voted me in."

"I'll ask them to vote you out!" Alyssa angrily flipped back her hair. "And I'll tell my aunt you're not good enough to be on the team."

Kathy's heart sank, but still she didn't back down. "I'll tell her I am. And I'll even show her!"

Alyssa gasped, suddenly looking at a loss for words. "You're going to be very sorry."

"No, Alyssa, I'm not sorry—I'm happy. You should be too. You're a great cheerleader, and you're popular in school."

Alyssa blinked in surprise. "Are you trying to be nice?"

Kathy giggled. "I am nice. I want you to know you don't have to be my enemy—or Brody's. He doesn't do drugs, and he doesn't sell them."

"So?"

"I just wanted you to know."

Alyssa scowled. "I don't believe you."

"Did you go to my house yesterday?"

"No! Why should I?"

Kathy could see Alyssa was telling the truth. "I just wondered." If Alyssa wasn't guilty of writing the note, who was? "Did you take something to my house?"

"I said I didn't go to your house. What does it matter anyway?"

Kathy shrugged. "I'll see you Monday at 2."

"The girls will vote you out."

Kathy shook her head. "No, they won't. We'll vote you out. What do you think of that?"

Alyssa's eyes widened in shock. "Vote *me* out?"

"Sure. And the girls will come to *my* house to practice. And we'll talk to your aunt and show her what we can do without you."

Alyssa knotted her fists at her sides, and her chest rose and fell. "Don't even try it."

"I won't unless you try to kick me out of the group. I like practicing with you because you're good and you know how to get us working together."

Alyssa bit her lip. "I guess you can stay in. But that doesn't mean I believe you about Brody."

"Well, it's true." Kathy rested her hands on her waist. "I hope you don't try to make him leave our house."

"I sure won't be nice to him if he comes near

me. I'll stay as far away from him as I can get."
Alyssa flipped her hair again, then ran to her house
and slipped inside.

Kathy slowly walked home. Who had sent the
note? Suddenly a terrible thought flashed in her
head. She gasped and pressed her hand to her heart.

Would Brody write the note himself knowing
the family would blame her? Did he hate her that
much?

Shivers ran up and down her back as she slowly
walked into her yard.

8

At the Zoo

Kathy laid two butter knives across the stack of white napkins on the picnic table to keep them from blowing away. She turned and watched Megan chase Brody around and around. He stayed just out of her reach, making her giggle so hard she could barely run. At the end of the table Duke poured punch into paper cups. Dad and Mom were taking the hotdogs and hamburgers off the grill. The smells made Kathy's stomach growl with hunger.

She looked around the crowded park. Grills stood in the green grass near tables lined with picnickers. Tall oaks and maples shaded the area. Bright red, orange, yellow, and gold flowers lined the walk that led to the gate of the zoo. Sounds of the lions roaring and the elephants trumpeting drifted into the park.

Kathy stuck a potato chip in her mouth. It was

salty and crunchy. She ate a slice of a dill pickle and wrinkled her face at the sour taste.

A flowered cup of punch in his hand, Duke walked to her side and said in a low, tight voice, "I thought I saw Cole Vangaar walk into the zoo."

Kathy trembled. "That's awful!"

"I could be wrong, but it sure looked like him . . . Long, dark, greasy hair, and shabby clothes."

"Oh my!"

"I didn't say anything to Brody. This is his first trip to the zoo, and I want him to have a good time."

"I didn't know he's never been to the zoo before." Kathy had been to the zoo two times a year for as long as she could remember. It seemed strange to think there was a person alive who hadn't been to the zoo. "Hasn't Brody ever seen wild animals?"

"No . . . Only pictures of them . . . And on TV, of course." Duke turned to watch Brody. Duke laughed as Megan finally caught Brody. "He's sure good with Megan. It would be terrible if Cole was here and did try to take Brody away."

Kathy shivered. "Dad wouldn't let that happen."

"Not if he could help it. I guess we'd better all stay close together today."

"You're right." Usually when they came to the zoo she and Duke would sometimes leave Mom and Dad with Megan and walk on alone. Megan always wanted to look at each animal a long, long time, like she was memorizing it or something.

Duke set his cup down and ran to Brody and Megan. "Wrestle him to the ground, Megan!"

Giggling, Kathy shook her head. Why did boys always want to wrestle? It would sure be funny if girls wrestled each other to the ground each time they met. Kathy laughed at the thought. Just then Brody glanced at her, then abruptly looked away. Her stomach tightened. She'd tried yesterday afternoon and last night to talk to him, but he wouldn't talk. Could he hate her enough to have written the note so she'd be blamed? She'd have to find out. But for now she'd rather believe he didn't do it.

"Come and eat, kids!" Dad called as he set the platter of burgers and hotdogs on the table beside the buns. Most of the red-checkered tablecloth was covered with food.

Breathing hard and damp with sweat, Megan ran to the table. "I'm hungry enough to eat everything on the table."

Kathy laughed. Duke usually said that. Megan was such a mimic.

Laughing, Brody and Duke raced to the table, both reaching it the same time.

"Let's pray before we fix our plates," Mom said.

Kathy bowed her head while Dad thanked God for the food and the beautiful day. When he said amen she lifted her head and met Brody's eyes. She smiled. His eyes widened, but then he looked away, his face as red as the catsup. Kathy locked her fingers together as her heart sank. Was it even possible to make friends with Brody?

"Come on, Kit Kat!" Dad held a flowered paper plate out to Kathy.

She hurried to him and took it with a smile. She would not give up on Brody so easily! She stabbed a hotdog with her plastic fork and put it between the bun. She squeezed a little mustard and catsup onto it, then spooned on diced onions. She took a bite. The onion was sweet and tasted good mixed with the tastes of the hotdog, mustard, and catsup. As she chewed she filled her plate with potato salad, potato chips, carrot sticks, one radish, and two bites of coleslaw. She walked along the table to the spot they'd kept clear for all of them to sit and eat. She started to sit beside Megan, then sat beside Brody instead. He looked at her with a startled look on his face, his mouth full of food.

"Kathy, can you reach a napkin for me?" Duke asked from Brody's other side.

"Sure." Kathy strained to reach the napkins. "Want one, Brody?"

He hesitated, then nodded.

Kathy picked up three napkins and gave one to Duke, one to Brody, and kept one for herself. Over the voices of Mom and Dad talking to Megan about the petting zoo, Kathy said, "I think you'll like seeing the monkeys, Brody. They're fun to watch jump and play. The baby ones are really cute." Kathy leaned forward and looked around Brody at Duke. "Aren't they, Duke?"

"Sure are. I like to see them clean bugs off each other."

"Yuk!" Kathy wrinkled her nose. "That's sick, Duke!"

Brody chuckled under his breath.

Kathy laughed. She took a bite of potato salad. It was full of eggs, just the way she liked it. She'd helped cut up the boiled potatoes and eggs last night. Dad had diced the onions because he liked them just right. He said if the pieces were too big, the flavor was too strong. She turned to Brody. "Do you like the potato salad?"

He choked on a bite, then nodded.

"I do too. The coleslaw's okay, but not my favorite. Mom loves it though." Brody didn't say anything, so Kathy ate in silence. She didn't want to push Brody too hard. He might snap at her. That would ruin everyone's day. She finished her plate, then fixed a hamburger and ate it. She dropped a potato chip and watched several ants try to pick it up. Across the park a baby cried. Inside the zoo a lion roared. The warm breeze blew the smell of grilled meat through the park.

"Kathy, did I hear your class is having a Sunday school party this week?" Mom asked.

Kathy nodded. "Tuesday night at the all-purpose room in the Sunday school wing. I'm supposed to take cookies."

"And Brody and I have to take punch or iced tea," Duke said. "We can each take a guest too."

"Take me!" Megan cried, bouncing on the seat beside Dad.

"Sorry," Dad said, "you're too young."

Megan stuck out her bottom lip in a pout, but Mom whispered something to her, and she smiled. Kathy knew Mom wouldn't allow Megan to pout.

"I'm not going," Brody said quietly.

"Sure, you are!" Duke punched Brody's arm. "You'll have fun. Won't he, Kathy?"

"Sure. You'd like the games and food, Brody."

Brody looked at Kathy, then quickly away. "I guess I'll go."

"Good." Kathy smiled. She was glad she was past her anger at Brody. Otherwise she would've been very upset to think about him being at the Sunday school party.

Several minutes later Kathy helped pack up the leftovers and load them in the station wagon. Finally it was time to go into the zoo. Brody was as excited as Megan. Kathy was glad she'd settled her dislike for Brody. Now she could have a good time.

Duke stepped close to Kathy and whispered,

"Be sure to watch for Cole. If you see him, tell me or Dad. He said not to say anything to Brody because it would ruin his day."

Kathy nodded. She wanted Brody to have fun. It would be fun just to watch Brody having a good time.

Dad paid their way into the zoo, and they walked into a wooded area with flowers, shrubs, and many different kinds of trees. An aviary stood just past a flower bed and a huge glass cage that held a bald eagle. The birds were loud, some with pretty songs and others with harsh noises. One bird sounded like the clap of a bell. Megan covered her ears as she looked at the different birds Mom pointed out. There were birds of every color, some beautiful and others drab. Kathy watched Brody look at the birds in awe. He nudged Duke and motioned to the parrots.

"They look just like the pictures I saw!" Brody laughed in delight. "They're so big! I'd hate to have one bite me."

"I bet it hurts." Duke watched a bright red and green parrot lean sideways on its perch. "I knew a kid who worked in a pet store. He said the parrot always pecked him when he cleaned the cage. He said it was like a hard pinch and turned him black and blue. He finally quit working there."

"I'd quit too." Brody hunched his shoulders as he watched the parrot.

"Not me!" Kathy shook her head. "I'd make friends with the parrot . . . or at least learn how to keep it from biting me."

"What if it kept biting you no matter what?" Brody asked.

Kathy's heart stopped, then pounded on. Brody had talked to her in a normal voice! "I'd keep trying."

Laughing, Duke jabbed Kathy's arm. "That's because you're stubborn."

"Or strong," Brody said.

Kathy lifted her chin. "You're right, Brody. I'm strong!"

Flushing, he ducked his head.

Smiling, Kathy walked out of the aviary and stopped at a glass cage with a dead tree branch in it. She looked, then jumped back. "It's a snake!"

Duke laughed. "You do that every time, Kathy. The snake can't hurt you, you know."

Kathy grinned sheepishly. "I know, but it's really scary to look at."

Brody touched the glass, then glanced at Kathy. "It can't get out."

Kathy held her breath. He'd talked to her again! Could it be he didn't hate her?

"Come on, Brody." Duke ran toward the next cage of snakes.

Kathy slowly followed. Mom, Dad, and Megan walked on ahead to the monkeys, with Megan chattering as usual. Crowds of people streamed past. Someone dropped popcorn, and it scattered across the sidewalk. A baby riding in a backpack cried. The sounds and smells all around were almost overwhelming.

Kathy glanced down the sidewalk that led to the petting zoo. She saw a man with long, greasy, dark hair. She froze. Was it Cole Vangaar? It sure looked like him. Trembling, she ran toward Duke, but he dashed away without noticing her. She didn't want to call him in case Cole—if it was Cole—heard her. She caught Brody's arm and tugged hard. "Let's go." Her voice was sharp, and she wished she would've kept it normal.

Brody jumped away from her, his eyes wide with alarm.

Chills ran up and down Kathy's spine even though it was warm. What was wrong with Brody? Did he think she was going to hurt him? "Let's catch up to Duke. Quick!"

Without a word Brody raced after Duke. Kathy followed close behind. She tried to get Duke alone to tell him she thought she'd seen Cole, but he was too involved with telling Brody about the monkeys and then the tigers. She tapped his arm. "Duke . . ."

He ignored her and kept talking to Brody.

Kathy finally gave up. Brody was far enough away from the petting zoo, so it didn't matter anyway. She relaxed and watched the tigers pace back and forth between the rocks to the tiny stream. They were sleek and beautiful.

Just then Megan ran to Brody. "Will you go to the petting zoo with me?"

Kathy gasped. She couldn't let Brody go there now. "I'll go with you, Megan. Brody wants to stay with Duke."

Brody frowned slightly. "I'll go with Megan. I told her I would."

"Well, you can't!" Kathy cried. "*I'm* going with her." Kathy turned to Duke. "Take him with you, Duke!" She knew she sounded frantic, but she couldn't help it.

Brody caught Megan's hand. "I said I'd go with her. Let's go!" He ran with her toward the petting zoo.

Kathy looked helplessly at Duke. "I saw Cole, I think, down by the petting zoo," she whispered urgently.

Duke raced after Brody. Kathy hesitated a second, then ran after him, dodging around a group of kids. She saw Duke catch up with Brody and try to talk to him. He kept going with Megan. Kathy's head spun. What could she do to keep Cole from seeing Brody? If the man wasn't Cole, there'd be no problem. But if he was—it would be awful!

Kathy ran around several people and up to Brody. She hesitated a second, then gripped his arm. "I want to show you the penguins. Megan, want to

see the penguins now and pet the baby animals
later?"

"What's wrong with you?" Brody growled.
"Leave us alone."

"Leave us alone," Megan mimicked.

Duke pulled Megan's ponytail. "Cut it out!
We're going to the penguins, and you're going with
us."

"We'll tell Dad if you don't," Kathy snapped.

"Why are you doing this?" Brody scowled at
Kathy. "What are you up to this time?"

"I want to see the penguins. We can pet the
baby animals later. Come on!" Kathy tugged him
toward the building where the penguins were
housed in special ice blocks and cold water.

Brody's face hardened. Without another word
he pulled away from her and walked with Duke
toward the penguins.

"What's wrong, Kathy?" Her eyes wide,
Megan looked up at Kathy.

"Nothing now." Kathy managed to smile.
"Let's go see the penguins. Remember, Megan?
They're the birds with black suits on, and they walk
funny."

"I remember!" Megan caught Kathy's hand
and ran after Brody and Duke.

Kathy breathed a sigh of relief. They'd kept
Brody away from danger. But what would happen

now if she tried to make friends with him? He was obviously very upset with her.

Stepping inside the building, Kathy looked for Brody. She saw him glance at her and then turn his back. She bit her lip and shivered. She'd thought she could make friends with Brody, but maybe she had ruined it by trying to keep him safe.

9

More Trouble

Her nerves tight, Kathy studied the crowd inside the petting zoo. A sturdy high wire fence circled the large grassy area. Many of the baby animals roamed free, while others were tied securely to one spot. With Mom and Dad beside her, Megan talked to a tiny donkey as she put her arms around its neck. Laughing, Brody watched Megan, then cautiously touched the donkey. He got braver and rubbed a hand along the donkey's black back. Several feet away Duke was petting a baby camel. Adults and children milled around the pen, looking at different animals.

His hands in the pocket of his jeans, Duke walked over to Kathy. "See him?"

"No. Did you?"

Duke shook his head. Suddenly his face turned as white as the clouds in the bright summer sky.

"Look! Just outside the fence near the petting zoo sign."

Kathy scanned the area. "I don't see him."

"He stepped behind a tree."

She sucked in her breath. "Are you sure it's Cole?"

"No . . . But he sure looks like Cole. Dad said he hadn't heard Cole was out of jail, but he said not to take any chances." Duke gripped Kathy's arm. "There he is!"

Kathy narrowed her eyes and studied the man Duke thought was Cole. "I just can't tell. Oh, he's looking this way! Duke, he looked right at me!" Kathy ducked her head and moved closer to Duke. "What's he doing now?"

"Walking away."

"Maybe Dad should call Officer Rodriguez and ask if Cole's out of jail."

"He tried, but he couldn't reach him. And nobody else would give Dad the information."

Kathy shivered. "Maybe we should go home."

"Dad says we're going to stay. He said not to worry, but just keep careful watch. He doesn't want to spoil the day for Brody or Megan." Duke hunched his shoulders. "I guess he knows we can handle it." Duke grinned. "It *is* pretty exciting. Almost like a thriller on TV."

Kathy frowned. "It's scary to me. I don't want Cole hurting any of us."

"There's too many people around for him to do that, Dad says. And I agree." Duke turned back to look at the animals. "Look at the baby goat, Kathy. It's so tiny!" He walked toward the gray and black goat and bent down to pet it.

Kathy saw a baby ostrich and walked slowly toward it just as Brody did. They reached it at the same time. It looked around with big round eyes. Kathy chuckled. "It's so ugly it's cute, isn't it?"

With a black look Brody backed away a step.

"I'm not going to hurt you," Kathy snapped. She opened her mouth to tell him they thought Cole was nearby, then closed it. Dad said not to tell, and she wouldn't.

Brody looped his thumbs in his belt. "Why are you even talking to me?"

Kathy hunched her shoulders. Her green blouse suddenly felt too hot. "I felt like it."

"You didn't before yesterday."

"I know. I'm sorry."

"Don't say it when you don't mean it." His face red, Brody turned and walked away. He stopped beside Mom and Dad and watched Megan pet a buffalo calf.

Tears burning her eyes, Kathy slowly walked to the gate. It was going to be a lot harder to make friends with Brody than it had been with Duke. But then, Duke hadn't hated her. He'd just ignored her.

For the next hour Kathy left Brody alone and

stayed close to Mom and Dad. She didn't spot Cole again—if it was Cole. In the station wagon driving home Kathy sat against the door with Duke beside her and Brody on the far side. She didn't say a word, and Brody did only when Duke asked him a question. But Megan, of course, chattered away, describing in great detail everything she'd seen as if no one else had been there.

At home Kathy walked slowly into the kitchen. The house was cool and seemed quiet after the noise of the park and zoo.

"I'm ready for some music!" Dad set the picnic basket on the counter and turned to the family. "We'll meet in the music room in fifteen minutes. Any objections?"

"Not a one." Mom hugged Dad. "I'm ready for music too . . . If it's not too loud, that is."

"The louder the better," Duke said with a grin. "Right, Brody?"

Brody nodded.

"I want to play the keyboard," Megan said, giggling.

"You don't know how." Dad lifted Megan high and swung her around. "But I'll teach you when you're a little bigger."

Kathy suddenly felt left out. She didn't know how to play any instrument either. Slowly she loaded the dirty dishes into the dishwasher while everyone helped clean up the picnic things. She wanted to call the Best Friends to get together with them, but she knew they were spending the day with their families too.

A few minutes later Kathy sat on the music room floor with her back against the leather sofa. Mom and Megan sat on the sofa. The boys bent over their guitars and tuned them to the piano. Dad plunked the note while the boys picked the right string and turned the tuner.

"You got it!" Dad laughed as he played a quick run on the piano. The joyful sound filled the room. He played a song Kathy didn't recognize, and the boys joined in on guitar.

Megan laid her head on Mom's lap and fell asleep. Mom smoothed Megan's hair back and smiled.

Kathy pulled her knees to her chin as she looked out the french doors into the backyard. She could see the edge of Megan's sandbox. A sparrow perched on the edge of the sandbox, then flew away. The swing set and the picnic table were out of Kathy's view.

Dad played another song, singing it as he played. It was a praise song he'd written himself.

Kathy hummed it under her breath. She knew some of the words but not enough to join in. Behind her she heard Mom singing quietly. She had a nice voice.

Later Kathy slipped out the french doors and

stood in the backyard. Mom and Dad had gone to take naps. Brody and Duke were playing Nintendo in the living room.

As Kathy walked across the backyard, a robin sang in a tree. The warm breeze blew the smell of boiled cabbage across the yard. Kathy wrinkled her nose as she walked around the house to the front door. She sat on the step with her chin in her hands. Nothing had worked out like she'd planned today. She'd wanted to be friends with Brody by the time they returned from the zoo, but things were worse than before. How could she make friends with Brody if he wouldn't even talk to her?

With a sigh Kathy walked to the kitchen door and slipped inside. She poured a glass of punch and drank it slowly as she leaned against the counter. She found a Hershey bar and ate it. The chocolate melted in her mouth and tasted delicious. In her bedroom she found a puzzle book and worked three puzzles. Impatiently she closed the book and stuffed it back in her drawer. She walked around her room, then out the door. Maybe the boys would let her play a video game with them.

She walked into the living room, then stopped short. It was empty. She hurried to the music room. It was empty too. She started to leave when the french doors opened and Brody rushed in. His face was dark with anger, and he held his guitar in his hand.

"How could you do this?" Brody held the guitar out to her.

"Do what?" She bit her lip. What had happened now?

"Scratch it! I came back to practice and found this!" He ran a trembling finger over the ugly scratch in the beautiful, shiny surface.

"But I didn't do that!"

"Who else did? Only you would! You were outside and knew when we left the room." Brody stood the guitar on its stand and faced Kathy again. "You want to be rid of me! I read the note you wrote, but I told your dad I hadn't because I didn't want you to get in trouble."

"But I didn't write the note!"

"Don't lie!"

"I don't lie, Brody. I didn't write the note, and I didn't scratch your guitar. Honest!" Kathy laced her fingers together. "But someone did. But who?" Could it be Alyssa? But how would she know which guitar belonged to Brody?

He shook his head. "I knew you didn't want me here."

Kathy flushed. "I didn't at first. But I was wrong!"

"I don't believe you."

"I don't lie! I want us to be friends. I really do." Kathy didn't know what else to say. Brody was too angry to listen to her. "You can ask Chelsea and Hannah and Roxie."

"Did you tell them how terrible it is to have me here?"

"Yes, but . . ."

"I knew it! Did you tell them I'm as bad as my brother?"

"No!"

"Did they tell you what to do to get rid of me?"

"Stop it, Brody! They told me how to make friends with you."

"That'll never happen in a million years!" Brody glared at Kathy.

"Don't say that!"

"Well, it's true!" He ran from the music room and down the hall.

Trembling, Kathy picked up Brody's guitar. Who had scratched it? If Cole was out of jail, would he do such a thing to make Brody angry enough to walk out?

Kathy set the guitar in place, then locked the french doors. She couldn't take a chance on someone coming in to do even more damage.

She stopped short. Maybe Brody had scratched the guitar himself. She pressed her hand to her mouth. He might want to get her in trouble no matter what he'd said. But would he do such a terrible thing to his beloved guitar?

Lifting her chin, Kathy marched out of the

103

room and straight to the bedroom Brody shared with Duke. The door was open, and she peered in, ready to confront Brody. The room was empty, and she felt as if someone had knocked all the air out of her.

Maybe he was in the living room again. She rushed down the hall and looked in the living room. It was empty, so she tried the kitchen. It was empty too. Where was Brody?

With determined steps Kathy walked to the study. The door was open, and she heard someone inside. Maybe it was Mom or Dad. Kathy peeked in. It was Brody, and he was going through the desk! Kathy bit back a gasp. None of them was ever allowed to go through the desk. What was he looking for? She waited and watched, her heart in her mouth. He closed the last drawer and slumped in the chair with a groan. He'd definitely been looking for something but hadn't found it. What could it be? Should she ask him? She couldn't find the courage to face him again.

Slowly Kathy walked back to the kitchen. She leaned against the counter and stared out the window. There was a real mystery here. She needed Hannah to help solve it.

Just then Duke ran into the kitchen. "Did you see Brody?"

"Why?"

"I just saw his guitar. Who would do such a thing?"

"Not me!"

"I didn't say you did. But you haven't been very nice to Brody—before last night, that is."

"Who would scratch his guitar? That's a terrible thing to do." Kathy laced her fingers together. "Duke, do you think Brody might do it himself?" She hesitated. "For some strange reason?"

"Never! That guitar is too important to him."

"It wasn't Megan. She's still asleep."

"Does Brody even know?"

Kathy nodded. "He thought I did it too."

"I didn't say I thought you did it!" Duke frowned. "I only wanted to know if you knew."

Kathy shook her head. "I plan to find out who did it. . . somehow."

"It's a mystery all right. Who would sneak into our house just to scratch Brody's guitar?"

Kathy started to say Alyssa might but stopped herself. She didn't want Duke to jump all over Alyssa if she weren't guilty.

"Maybe Cole's been sneaking around here and did it to make Brody leave." Duke rubbed his cheek just like Dad did when he was worried. "Dad's going to call tomorrow to see if Cole is out of jail. I sure hope he's not!"

What would happen to them if Cole *was* out of jail? Kathy shivered and stepped closer to Duke.

A Real Mystery

Kathy sat on the green park bench and watched Megan playing catch with another little girl. They had a big red ball and caught it only twice out of ten throws. They giggled every time they missed, then would both race to it.

Kathy bit her lip as she thought about what Dad had told her and Duke a while ago. He'd called Officer Rodriguez before breakfast and learned that Cole Vangaar was still in jail. Yesterday they'd been frightened for nothing. Kathy sighed. Since Cole was still in jail, she could check off one suspect. Alyssa and Brody were the only two left.

But what if someone she'd never thought of was guilty of writing the note and scratching the guitar? She frowned and helplessly shook her head. That made the mystery too hard to solve.

Who could've done it? An old enemy of

Brody's? A new enemy? The entire population of Middle Lake?

Just then Mike McCrea ran up to Kathy. His face and hair were damp with sweat. He wore bright orange shorts and shirt. "Sorry I'm late." He wiped his face off. "I had to help Rob finish sweeping the garage."

"That's all right. I'm not feeling much like practicing anyway."

"So what?" Mike grinned as he tugged on her hand. "That's what my teacher always said to me. You have to practice to be good even when you don't feel like it. So get up and practice. Stretch your muscles, then do flips."

Laughing, Kathy securely tucked her gold T-shirt into her gray shorts. Megan was playing in the sandbox and would probably stay there the rest of the time. "If Megan leaves the sandbox, tell me, Mike."

"I will."

Kathy stretched her muscles, took a deep breath, and flipped back and forth in the soft grass. She felt as if her arms were springs as she landed on her hands, then shot up and over to land on her feet, then over on her hands and back to her feet. She could tell she was getting better.

"Very good, Kathy. Now do cartwheels," Mike called.

Kathy ran, pressed her hands to the ground,

and lifted her legs high. She did five, ending the last one beside Mike. She wiped sweat off her face and smiled proudly.

"Real good, Kathy." Mike smiled. "Want me to show you anything else?"

"Not today." Kathy dropped to the bench and let the breeze cool her off. "Thanks for your help."

"Sure." Grinning, Mike sat beside her. "Thanks for talking Brody into teaching me guitar."

"I didn't talk him into it."

"He said you did."

Kathy shook her head. "I only said you wanted him to teach you."

Mike shrugged. "I'm glad he is. I want to be as good in guitar as I am in gymnastics. A pro . . . Like your dad . . . And like Brody."

"Somebody scratched Brody's guitar yesterday." The words popped out before she knew they were coming. She wanted to take them back, but it was too late.

"You're kidding! Who'd do such a rotten thing?"

"I don't know. He thought I did it."

"You'd never do that."

"That's what I told him. But we can't figure out who would've."

"I hope he never thinks I did it." Mike rubbed his hands down his shorts. "He wouldn't ever think that, would he?"

"I doubt it. Besides, you weren't at our house yesterday in the late afternoon, were you?"

"No."

"So you're not even a suspect."

Mike grinned. "A suspect! Just like on TV." He sobered. "I don't know who would scratch his guitar. That's really sad. He loves that guitar!"

"Who even knows about his guitar besides our family and you?"

"Probably your neighbors."

"Mrs. Sobol wouldn't do it. Nor would the Thomsons or the Heinzes. But Alyssa Carroll might."

"She gave me a note to leave at your house."

Kathy almost jumped out of her skin. "When?"

"Friday when I was there for a lesson. She was standing in your backyard, and she asked if I'd take it and leave it on the piano. So I did."

Alyssa had written the note! Kathy could barely sit still.

Mike frowned. "Do you think she scratched the guitar?"

"I don't know." Kathy's heart beat so hard, she was sure Mike could hear it. "But I'll find out." She started toward Megan. "Thanks for your help, Mike. I'm going home now."

"See you in the morning."

Kathy smiled and nodded. It was hard to think of anything but Alyssa Carroll.

Several minutes later Kathy left Megan with Mom in the study. "I'm going to see Alyssa."

Mom looked up from hugging Megan. "It's not two o'clock, Kathy. What's up?"

"I need to talk to her."

Mom shrugged. "Let me know when you get back."

Kathy nodded, then slowly walked to the kitchen. Her mouth suddenly felt cotton-dry. She filled a glass with cold water and drank it almost in one gulp. Should she call the Best Friends and tell them what was happening? Nodding, she reached for the phone, then remembered they all had jobs this morning.

Trembling, Kathy walked to Alyssa's house. A cloud drifted over the sun. Mom had said there was a chance of rain today. Kathy looked up at the sky. "Don't rain until after practice," she muttered. She stopped, her hand at her throat. Maybe there wouldn't be any practice for her after she talked to Alyssa. Too bad! She had to talk to her no matter what.

Taking a deep breath, Kathy walked past the red geranium and knocked on Alyssa's front door.

The door opened, and Alyssa stood there with a scowl on her pretty face. "What are you doing here?"

"We need to talk."

Alyssa looked over her shoulder into the house,

then stepped out and closed the door. "I talked to my aunt and told her everything you said. She said you wouldn't have a chance as a cheerleader with that kind of attitude."

Kathy's nerves tightened. Was Alyssa telling the truth? "I didn't come to talk about cheerleading."

"Oh." Alyssa sounded disappointed.

"It's about the note you wrote and had Mike McCrea leave on our piano."

Alyssa trembled, then stiffened her back and lifted her chin. "What note?"

"It won't do any good to lie about it. I just want you to know Brody does not do drugs, and he is not leaving our house. He's part of the family now." Kathy couldn't bring herself to say he was her new brother.

Alyssa pressed her lips tightly together.

"Nothing you do will make him leave," Kathy went on.

"But *you* could make him leave! And you're going to if you want me to tell my aunt you've changed your bad attitude."

"I'll talk to her myself!"

"Well, you can't! She has an unlisted phone number, and I won't tell you what it is. And I won't tell you her married name. The school won't either. What now, Kathy A Teddy Bear?"

Kathy's temper started to rise, but she forced it

down. "I'll talk to the other girls. They'll come to *my* house to practice and leave you out."

Alyssa looked very pleased with herself. "I already told them just what I told you, and they won't take your side against me. So there!"

Kathy bit back a long line of bad names she wanted to call Alyssa. Jesus didn't want her to call Alyssa names. "I'll be at practice at 2."

"Fine. But if you don't do just what I say, you're out!" Alyssa jerked the door open and slipped inside.

Kathy slowly walked down the steps past the red geranium and onto the sidewalk. She stopped short. She'd forgotten to see if Alyssa had scratched Brody's guitar. "I'll find out later," she muttered as she started walking again. But she'd be very careful how she went about it. She wouldn't give Alyssa any reason to kick her off the practice team before she found a way to talk to Alyssa's aunt and tell her the truth.

Back home Kathy hesitated outside the music room. Brody was practicing. He sat on the chair bent over his guitar as he strummed chord after chord. Duke had gone to school to sign up for wrestling. He'd worked hard all summer to build up his strength and to keep his weight right.

Kathy took one step inside the music room. "Brody?"

He turned his head, frowned, and turned back

to his guitar. The sound was beautiful even though the shiny wood was scratched.

Kathy bit her lip, hesitated, then walked right up to Brody. "I just learned from Mike McCrea that he brought the note Friday. It was from Alyssa Carroll. Her cousin died because he took drugs Cole sold to him. So Alyssa is mad at you." Kathy waited for Brody to speak or look up. He did neither. "She wanted me to do something to make you leave, and I refused. I said you're here to stay."

Brody slowly looked up. "I don't even know Alyssa Carroll."

"I know."

"Isn't she the girl you cheerlead with?"

Kathy nodded.

"So why don't you quit if she's that kind of girl?"

"I want to be a cheerleader. Her aunt chooses the girls on the team."

Brody slowly stood his guitar on the stand. He walked to the french doors and looked out, then turned to Kathy. "Did you really tell her you want me to stay?"

Kathy nodded.

"Did you mean it?"

"Yes."

Brody's eyes lit up. "I thought you hated me."

Kathy flushed. "I never hated you. I just didn't want another brother. But I was wrong, and I asked

Jesus to forgive me . . . And I want you to forgive me."

"There's nothing to forgive."

Kathy licked her lips. "Do you . . . hate me?"

Brody's eyes widened in surprise. "No! I think you're great." He blushed scarlet. "I *never* hated you."

Kathy breathed a sigh of relief. She laughed softly. "Thanks. Maybe now we can act like brother and sister."

"I'd like that. I never had a sister." Brody grinned. "Now I have two!"

Kathy glanced at Brody's guitar. "We still have to find out who scratched your guitar."

Brody ran his finger over the ugly scratch. "Was it Alyssa?"

"It could've been."

Brody knotted his fists. "I'll get her for it!"

"No! No, Brody. You shouldn't try to get even. Jesus says not to."

A muscle in Brody's jaw jumped. "You're right. But it's sure hard."

"I know." Kathy told him what she'd gone through and how the Best Friends had helped her.

Brody sank to his chair. "You have good friends. I never had a friend before I met Duke."

"Now you have me. And Megan too." Kathy realized she actually liked Brody. She hadn't expected to.

"So what'll we do about Alyssa?"

"We'll find a way to show her you're a nice guy. And we'll show her aunt I'm a good cheerleader. I don't know how we'll do it, but we will."

Just then the kitchen door slammed, and Duke shouted, "I'm home! Mom?"

"Sounds like he made the wrestling team," Kathy said with a laugh. "Let's go see." She hurried to the kitchen with Brody close behind her. It felt good to finally be friends with him.

Duke stood in the kitchen, talking excitedly to Mom and Megan.

"Did you make it?" Brody asked.

Duke lifted his arms and flexed his muscles. "Of course! Who wouldn't want this power team?"

Kathy giggled as Brody and Duke scuffled around the kitchen in mock combat.

Mom turned to Kathy. "You got a call for a *King's Kid* job a few minutes ago. I told Chelsea you'd call her."

"Thanks, Mom. Is she home?"

"Yes. Until noon."

Kathy hurried to the study, perched on the edge of the chair, and quickly dialed the phone. The boys were too noisy for her to use the kitchen phone. Chelsea answered on the first ring. "What do you have for me, Chel?"

"A perfect job for you, Kath." Chelsea laughed

softly. "Mrs. Carroll needs someone to work in her backyard."

Kathy froze. "Mrs. Carroll? Alyssa's mom?"

"Yup. She's going to have an outdoor party and needs special work done."

Was Chelsea teasing? "Alyssa Carroll's mom?"

"Uh huh. Isn't this perfect for letting them know Brody's okay?"

"How?"

"You can take Brody with you and let her see what an excellent job he does. Just be sure Mrs. Carroll knows who Brody is."

"I don't know about this, Chel."

"It'll work! Do it, will you?"

"I guess. Oh, Chel, I don't know if I really can do this!"

"Sure, you can. This really is absolutely perfect, Kath!"

The more Kathy thought about it, the better she liked it. "I guess you're right."

"Of course I am!"

"It's pretty scary, Chel."

"If you don't want to do it, I'll assign someone else."

Kathy wanted to tell her to do just that, but she didn't. She knew it was a good opportunity she shouldn't let slip through her fingers. "No. That's all right. I'll do it. And Brody too."

"Good. How's it going with you and Brody?"

Kathy smiled. "We had a great talk and we're— well—almost friends— I mean, we're friends."

"I love it! I'll let you tell the others the good news. But it'll be hard. You know how I like telling things." Chelsea giggled. "See ya later."

"See ya." Kathy hung up, then sagged back in the chair. Could they really show Mrs. Carroll that Brody wasn't like his brother Cole?

Just then the picture of Brody looking through the desk flashed across Kathy's mind. She touched the top drawer.

"What was he after?" she whispered with a shiver.

11

An Important Job

Her heart thundering, Kathy stood at the back door of Alyssa's house. "Are you scared, Brody?"

He nodded. "Are you?"

"A little." Could she really stay, or would she run home and hide?

The door opened, and Mrs. Carroll smiled. She was medium build with blonde hair and blue eyes. She wore jeans and a pink plaid blouse. "Kathy! I was at my wit's end trying to find someone to help me!" Her smiled wavered as she looked at Brody.

"This is my new brother, Brody. He's a good worker."

"I'm sure he is." Mrs. Carroll looked flustered, but she didn't send Brody away. She showed them the flagstone patio and the sidewalk that led around the house. "Pull the weeds out of the cracks. Mow the grass. Trim the edges. Rake. Be sure to pick up the twigs. Put the toys in the garage. My two youngest never remember to take care of their things." Mrs. Carroll spread her hands. "Oh, I don't know! Just make it look nice. You have such a short time. I'll send Alyssa out to help when she gets home. She took the children to the baby-sitters for the night, but she'll help you when she returns."

Kathy darted a look at Brody. They hadn't expected that. She wanted to say it wasn't necessary, but she didn't want to make trouble. At 2 she'd practiced with Alyssa and the girls without any problem.

"Well, you kids get to work. I hope you're done before 5."

"Oh, we will be," Kathy said.

Brody nodded. "We're hard workers."

"If you have any questions, knock on the back door. I'll be working in the kitchen." Mrs. Carroll sighed and brushed back her shoulder-length hair. "I surely could use help making the special cookies I want to serve tonight."

"Call Chelsea McCrea. She'll send someone right over."

Mrs. Carroll beamed. "I'll do just that! Thank you, Kathy. You're a sweet child."

"Thank you." Kathy blushed. She hated being called "a sweet child."

"The tools are in the garage. You do know how to use a lawn mower, don't you?"

"Yes," Kathy answered just as Brody did.

Probably Alyssa didn't know how, so Mrs. Carroll was surprised others her age did.

A few minutes later Brody pulled weeds while Kathy picked up twigs, toys, and some really awful piles of dog manure. She rolled the lawn mower out of the garage, started it with a roar, and mowed the lawn while Brody edged the sidewalk and the patio. When he finished edging, he raked with a leaf rake where Kathy had mowed. She looked around the backyard proudly as she took the last turn with the mower. It was looking great, and they were done before the deadline.

Just then Alyssa stepped out on the lawn with a wad of white paper towels in her hand. She made a face at Kathy and tossed the balled paper towels directly in front of the lawn mower. Kathy couldn't help running over the wad, sending pieces of paper flying over the tidy lawn, turning it white in spots. She stopped the mower and faced Alyssa angrily. "Look what you did! And we were almost finished!"

Alyssa shrugged. "Now you have more work to do. Doesn't that mean more money for you two *King's Kids*?" With a sneer she walked back inside.

"She's a brat!" Brody said with a scowl. "I don't know how you can stand her."

"Actually I can't." Kathy hung her head. "I'm sorry . . . I am trying to learn to love others with God's love."

"Even Alyssa?"

"It seems impossible, doesn't it? But it's not." Kathy waved a hand at the scattered paper towel. "Let's get it cleaned up before Mrs. Carroll sees it and gets upset."

Just then the back door opened, and Mrs. Carroll burst out with Alyssa right behind her. "What in the world happened? Alyssa told me Brody deliberately threw a wad of paper in the mower."

"That's not true," Kathy said softly. "We'll get it raked up quickly though."

"Then who did do it?" Mrs. Carroll snapped.

Kathy shrugged, and Brody pressed his lips tightly together.

"So you're not talking. Well, I don't have time for this. Alyssa, come help me in the kitchen."

"But you hired Hannah to help you. Let her do it."

Kathy tried to catch a glimpse of Hannah through the kitchen window but couldn't see her.

Mrs. Carroll frowned at Alyssa and hurried back inside.

Alyssa stepped up to Kathy. "Why didn't you tell on me?"

Kathy lifted her chin. "We aren't tattletales."

"Your mom is too tense about the party to learn you did such a mean thing," Brody said. "You should think about her instead of yourself."

Alyssa spun around and stormed inside, slamming the door.

"She's mad." Brody grinned. "She expected you to say she did it, so she could call you a liar."

"I didn't think of that." Kathy pulled the rake over the lawn and soon had the toweling in a pile that Brody picked up. She started the mower with a roar and quickly finished the lawn. Her arms vibrated with the bounce and roar. She shut off the engine and wheeled the mower back into the garage. "Let's see if Mrs. Carroll needs help setting up tables and chairs."

"Why?"

"*King's Kids* always do more than they're asked to do."

"That's good."

With Brody beside her, Kathy knocked on the door. "You ask her, Brody."

"Me? Why?"

"I want her to know you're okay."

Brody grinned. "As long as you think so, that's enough for me."

Kathy smiled and jabbed his arm. "Cut it out, you."

Mrs. Carroll opened the door, a harried look on her face.

Brody smiled. "We're done, but we wondered if you need us to set up tables and chairs for you."

Mrs. Carroll gasped in surprise. "You are

dears! I mean it! Yes, please do. They're right inside here. Put them on the patio in such a way that we can walk all the way around them comfortably and still be on the patio."

"We'll do it," Brody said with a nod. He walked to the folding table.

Kathy lifted one end and Brody the other. They carefully set the table up on the patio so the legs weren't near the cracks of the flagstones. They set the chairs in place around the table, then set three of them off to one side. "Looks good," Brody said.

Alyssa stepped onto the patio. "Mom says come inside and she'll pay you."

"Thanks," Kathy said, smiling.

Alyssa turned abruptly away and walked back in.

With Brody close behind her, Kathy hurried after Alyssa to the kitchen. Hannah looked up from taking cookies off a cookie sheet.

"Hi." Hannah smiled. Two braids hung down her shoulders on her yellow T-shirt. Her *I'm A Best Friend* button was pinned in place on her chest.

"Smells good in here," Kathy said.

Mrs. Carroll pulled some money out of her purse.

"You owe us only for two hours," Brody said. "We set up the table and chairs just to help you out."

"Oh . . . well, I don't know what to say." Mrs.

Carroll looked from one to the other as if she couldn't believe her ears.

"He's right." Kathy smiled. "If there's anything else, let us know and we'll help."

"Well, no, that's all." Mrs. Carroll paid them for the two hours, then hurried away to answer the phone.

Alyssa looked from Kathy to Brody and back again. "That good deed won't get you onto the cheerleading team."

"We didn't do it for that reason." Kathy turned to Hannah. "Stop in before you go home, will you?"

"Sure. It'll be soon. This is the last batch of cookies."

"See you then." Kathy started for the door. She looked over her shoulder at Alyssa. "Have fun at the party."

"Yeah, sure. I don't have any friends coming."

"That's too bad." Kathy glanced at Brody. "Want us to come? Brody could bring his guitar."

Alyssa flushed and shook her head.

From behind them Mrs. Carroll said, "Brody, do you play guitar?"

Brody nodded.

"He's very good," Kathy said.

"Mom!" Alyssa cried.

Mrs. Carroll ignored Alyssa as she smiled at Brody. "Could you bring your guitar and play for us tonight? About 8?"

Brody shrugged. "I'll ask my foster dad, but he'll probably let me."

"Oh, this is wonderful!" Mrs. Carroll beamed. "The guests will be so pleased."

Kathy glanced at Hannah, and they smiled at each other.

"Kathy, you're welcome to come with him," Mrs. Carroll said. "You'll help keep Alyssa from being bored."

"Thank you. We'll call you to let you know that it's all right with our folks." Kathy said good-bye to Hannah and Alyssa and walked out with Brody close behind her.

On the sidewalk leading to their house Brody laughed. "I can't believe it! I'm going to be the entertainment tonight! And for a family that doesn't like me!"

"It's great! Dad and Mom will be glad too."

Later Kathy sat in the backyard with Hannah beside her on the picnic table.

"I learned where Alyssa's aunt lives," Hannah announced with pride.

Kathy cried out in delight. "How'd you do that?"

"I talked to Mrs. Carroll, and she told me. Alyssa doesn't know she told me." Hannah grinned. "Pamela Brewer is her name now, and she lives in The Ravines near Nick Rand."

"I can't believe it! That's great!" Pamela

Carroll had gotten married in July, and none of the students knew her new name or where she lived. But now Kathy knew, thanks to Hannah. It was the best news she'd heard all week.

"So we'll make sure you get to talk to her and even show her what you can do." Hannah jumped off the table. "I have to get home. See you tomorrow night at the Sunday school party."

"I'll tell you how tonight goes. It should be very interesting." Kathy walked Hannah to her bike and waved to her as she pedaled away.

Just before eight o'clock Kathy smiled at Brody, dressed in nice jeans and a pink shirt with his guitar hung over his shoulder. She wore her new jeans and a pullover pink and red top.

Mom looked them over. "You both look great. You can stay only an hour. But if they start drinking, come right home."

"We will," Kathy said.

A few minutes later Kathy and Brody walked into the Carrolls' backyard. Smells of grilled steaks still hung in the air. Men and women were laughing and talking. Mrs. Carroll spotted Brody and called him to her.

"Our music is here now . . . Brody Vangaar, foster son of the Abers. I hear he plays almost as well as Tommy Aber."

At the sound of the applause, Kathy joined Alyssa at the edge of the patio. "Hi."

"I didn't think you'd come."

"I called your mom and said we would."

Alyssa shrugged. "Why would you bother? You don't even like me."

"Only because you won't let me."

"What do you mean by that?"

"You're always snapping at me or making fun of me. Why can't we just talk like normal girls do? I know you like sports, and so do I. You like music, and so do I."

"Brody's playing. I want to hear just how good he is. I still can't believe my dad let him come."

Brody strummed the guitar, and everyone grew quiet. Kathy swelled with pride. He played several of the songs Dad had taught him. After each song the people clapped and cheered. Kathy wondered if they knew all the songs were Christian songs.

"He *is* good," Alyssa whispered. "I saw him through the french doors, but I didn't know he was so good."

Kathy stared at Alyssa. "Why did you scratch his guitar?"

Alyssa ducked her head. "I can't believe I did such a mean thing! But I was so angry at his brother for what he did to my cousin that when I saw a chance to sneak into your house, I did. I was going to smash Brody's guitar to pieces, but I knew that would make too much noise. I started to put it back on the stand and saw how easy it would be to scratch it with the edge of the stand. So I did."

"Brody thought I did it."

"That's what I wanted him to think."

"I convinced him I didn't. We both figured you did it."

Alyssa nervously brushed back her hair. "But you didn't tell my folks. How come?"

"We didn't want to get you in trouble with them."

"Oh, sure. What's the real reason? Because of my aunt and getting on the cheerleading team?"

"No. Besides, Brody doesn't want to be on the team." Kathy giggled. "He'd hate being a cheerleader."

Alyssa laughed, the first laugh Kathy had heard from her in a long time.

"You're different than I thought you'd be," Alyssa said.

"Oh?"

"I know you're a Christian. I guess I thought you'd try to preach to me or something."

"I will if you want. Jesus does love you. He knows all about you and wants to be your Friend and your Savior."

Alyssa sighed. "I know. Dad makes fun of that."

"Only because he doesn't know Jesus loves him."

Alyssa brushed a tear from her eye. "Let's listen to Brody. It makes me cry to have you talk about . . . about Jesus. I don't know why."

"Because you want Him as your friend."

"Maybe. But I'm not saying I do!"

Kathy smiled. "Let's listen to Brody. He's good all right. And he's a great brother." But once again she thought of him going through the desk in the study, and the tiny doubt grew a little bigger.

She watched as he ended the last song, stood, and bowed. She clapped with everyone else, then stood to go. "See you tomorrow, Alyssa."

"Sure . . . I guess."

Smiling, Brody hung his guitar over his back and walked over to Kathy. Mrs. Carroll called to him, and he turned to face her.

"What do I owe you, Brody?"

He flushed. "I don't know. I didn't know you planned to pay me."

"But of course I'll pay you!" Mrs. Carroll laughed as she handed Brody twenty dollars. "You keep on with your guitar. You have real talent."

"Thank you."

Kathy smiled with pride.

"Why, look at that scratch!" Mrs. Carroll ran her finger over the scratch. "I hope you didn't do that here tonight."

Brody darted a look at Alyssa, then shook his head. "It was already like that."

"Well, good night to both of you." Mrs. Carroll smiled, then turned back to her guests.

"Goodnight, Alyssa," Brody said.

"Bye," she whispered.

Kathy fell into step with Brody, and they slowly walked home. "You were really good tonight, Brody."

"Thanks. I make a few mistakes."

"I didn't hear them, and I don't think anyone else did either."

"It was fun. And I got paid for it." He chuckled and shook his head. "Now I know how your dad feels when he gets paid for doing something he loves to do."

Just then Alyssa ran up behind them. "Brody, I'm sorry I scratched your guitar." She sounded close to tears. "Take this to help pay for the repair." She held out a twenty dollar bill.

He hesitated, and she stuffed it in his shirt pocket, then turned and ran back to her house.

"What a shock," he said, watching her run.

"I'm glad she did it. It'll make her feel better." Kathy smiled as she turned back toward home. This had been a very surprising day. She couldn't wait to tell the Best Friends all that had happened. But what would they think when she told them about Brody going through the desk drawers?

12

The Sunday School Party

Kathy looked excitedly around the all-purpose room for the Best Friends. They'd agreed they'd try to play on the same teams if possible. The room was decorated with bouquets of bright balloons. In one corner a popcorn machine was warming up to begin its popping. In a room already crowded with boys and girls, tables were set up for board games. A big space in the middle of the room was empty for team games. Duke had taken Brody to the area where a group of boys was playing. As she looked around, Kathy spotted Justine Gold. She wore pale blue slacks and a white-and-blue pullover top. Kathy hurried toward her with a welcoming smile. She'd invited Justine to be her guest but hadn't really expected her to come. "Hi! I'm glad you came."

Justine licked her lips nervously. "I almost didn't."

"Well, I'm happy you did! Come meet everyone."

Justine glanced around. "I see a lot of kids I know from school."

"Great! Let's go say hi."

"Wait. Do you know why Alyssa canceled cheerleading practice today?"

Kathy shook her head. "I thought it might be because of the party last night. Maybe she had to help clean up or something."

"She wouldn't have to help." Justine twisted a strand of hair around her finger. "Maybe she's going to get other girls to practice with."

"No. Besides, who's as good as we are?" Kathy grinned. "Don't worry about it, Justine. I know where Alyssa's aunt lives, and I plan to talk to her myself."

"Oh my!"

Just then Chelsea ran up, her red hair bouncing around her slender shoulders. "Hi, Kath."

"Chelsea, this is Justine."

"Glad to meet you, Justine. Want to play Pictionary?"

Justine looked helplessly at Kathy.

"Sure, let's play it," Kathy said confidently.

Justine shrugged. "I'm not that good."

"Be my partner. I almost always win." Kathy

giggled as she walked to the table with Justine and Chelsea. Pam, Mona, and Lora were already there.

Kathy explained to Justine what some basic drawings meant in the game, and then they started. She and Justine had the red piece.

Chelsea and Lora went first. Pam flipped the timer, and Mona said, "Go!" Chelsea drew a statue, and Lora guessed it before ten grains of sand slipped through the timer.

The next turn was an all play. Holding her pencil on the paper, Kathy smiled at Justine. Pam said, "Go!" and Kathy quickly drew her sloppy version of the United States. The state of Texas looked like a lump. The word was New York City. She pointed to where New York was, but Justine couldn't guess it.

"New York City!" Chelsea cried.

"Oh!" Justine shook her head and groaned. "I thought that was it, but I was afraid to guess."

"Never be afraid!"

Justine drew the next picture, and Kathy guessed it before anyone else. They won the turn, rolled the dice, and moved their marker four spaces.

"Good going, Justine," Kathy said as she drew a card from the box. "We're a good team."

Justine laughed and for the first time looked relaxed.

Kathy waited for Pam to turn the timer over,

then quickly drew a tree. Justine guessed it immediately. "You roll this time," Kathy said.

Justine rolled a six and moved the marker. "I like this game!"

"Me too." Kathy laughed as she leaned toward Justine to see her drawing.

Across the room a boy shouted, "Brody Vangaar has drugs on him!"

Kathy whirled around and stared in shock across the room. Was someone making a horrible joke? But she could tell by Brody's face it wasn't a joke. She dashed across to Brody just as Duke reached him. "What's going on?" Kathy whispered while a million eyes bored into her.

Brody groaned. "Somebody dropped two little red pills next to my foot and said they fell from my pocket."

Duke frowned at the group. "Who would do that to Brody? Sam, do you know?"

"I didn't see nothing." Sam stepped back and bumped into another boy. "Honest, Duke, I didn't see nothing."

Kathy felt Brody tremble. Was he guilty? Maybe he did do drugs and had been keeping it a secret from the whole family.

Just then Linda Huron and Steve Perry, the Sunday school teachers of the sixth and seventh grades, rushed to the crowd gathered around Brody. The kids grew quiet and stared at Linda and Steve.

"Is something wrong?" Steve looked around the group. He was almost thirty years old with dark hair and eyes. His short-sleeved blue shirt strained over his thick middle and was tucked neatly into his jeans. "Duke?"

"Somebody accused Brody of having drugs." Duke's voice broke, and he took a deep breath. "But he's not guilty."

Steve took the red heart-shaped pills that could've been acid. "They look like candy," he said.

Linda patted Brody on the arm. "I'm sure we'll get this all cleared up." She glanced at the others. "Go back to playing games or whatever while we take care of this . . . Please."

Nobody moved. Kathy wanted to, but she couldn't get her legs to obey.

Over the voices of others around them, Chelsea tugged on Kathy's arm and whispered, "Come on."

"You go ahead. I want to stay with Brody."

"I should've listened to Alyssa," Justine said sharply. "She warned me about Brody."

Kathy scowled at Justine. "Don't say anything against him!"

Justine bit her lip and walked away with her head down.

Kathy turned back to listen to the teachers talking to Brody. They sounded like they thought Brody was guilty! Kathy trembled. Maybe she should call Dad to come help. Yes, that's just what she'd do! She whispered her plan to Duke and hurried around the crowd to a phone in the hall. She called Dad and breathlessly explained what was happening. "I know he's innocent, Dad."

"Me too, Kit Kat. See you in a few minutes."

Kathy hung up and leaned weakly against the wall. Would the others ever believe the truth? But what was the truth? She groaned from deep inside.

"Kathy?"

At the sound of Hannah's soft voice she looked up. Hannah, Roxie, and Chelsea stood there, looking concerned for her. Tears filled her eyes.

Chelsea caught Kathy's hand. "Let's go outside and talk."

"I should be in there with Brody."

"Steve and Linda took him and Duke to the office. They're going to call your dad," Roxie said.

"I already did." Kathy stepped outside and lifted her face to the cool breeze. It was still light out, but the sun was down, and much of the heat had gone out of the day. A motorcycle roared past, breaking the silence. Gradually the sound died out, and the silence returned.

"Please don't worry, Kathy." Hannah's black eyes were wide in her dark face. She had a broad forehead and high cheekbones.

"We'll stay with you," Roxie said.

Kathy glanced anxiously toward the door. "What happened to Justine?"

"She found a girl she knew and sat with her," Chelsea answered.

Kathy brushed her hand over her eyes. "What if Brody did have drugs? It would be awful!"

"He said he didn't." Chelsea turned to Hannah. "Didn't he?"

"Yes. And I believe him."

"We all believe him," Roxie said.

Just then Kathy saw Dad stop his car at the end of the sidewalk. He ran toward the door. His jeans seemed extra-loose on his lean frame. He spotted her and stopped.

"Daddy, they have Brody in the office!" Kathy flung herself against Dad and held him tightly.

Dad hugged her and kissed the top of her blonde curls. "Stay with your friends while I go talk to them. It's going to be all right, Kit Kat. God's with us."

Kathy felt as if a weight had lifted off her. She smiled as she watched Dad run inside the Sunday school wing of the church.

"He looks different without his ponytail," Hannah said.

"I'm glad he had his hair cut." Kathy slowly walked toward the church. "Some people made fun of him."

"I'd be embarrassed if my dad had long hair." Roxie held the door open for the others. "Once he said he was going to let it grow and pull it back in a ponytail. I cried and cried. He told me he was only teasing. I sure was glad."

"Parents sometimes do embarrassing things," Chelsea said as she closed the door behind all of them. Laughter rang out from the all-purpose room. The smell of hot buttered popcorn overpowered all other smells.

Kathy locked her fingers together and looked down the wide hall. "I want to go to the office."

"Your dad said to stay with us," Hannah said. "We could go play a game."

Chelsea pointed down the hall. "Or wait in the alcove down the hall."

"Let's do that." Kathy hurried down the hall, her sneakers quiet on the gray tile. She sank to the yellow armchair and crossed her legs. It felt like a lead ball was stuck in her stomach.

Chelsea and Hannah sat on a leather-covered bench facing Kathy. Roxie pulled a chair up close. Kathy felt as if they were all gathering around her to keep her from harm or danger. They were her friends, her best friends.

Chelsea wrapped her hands around her knees. "I think my worst time of waiting was when my mom and dad had a big argument back in Oklahoma, and my dad walked out. I didn't think he was ever coming back. But he did, and he even apologized for leaving. He said he'd never do it again, and he didn't." Chelsea shivered. "It was really scary. I wouldn't want to have him do it again. Mom wouldn't either. She cried and cried. I didn't know what to say to her."

Roxie gripped the arms of her chair. "My worst time of waiting was when Mom went to the hospital to have Faye. A girl at school said moms sometimes die when they have babies. I was sooo afraid Mom might die. I cried and cried. Dad thought I was just jealous since I wasn't going to be the youngest any longer. I wanted to tell him why I was so upset, but I just couldn't. But Mom came home with Faye." Roxie brushed a tear off her cheek. "I was glad."

Hannah hooked her hair behind her ears. "The time my dad was arrested just because he's Ottawa and was near a service station that was robbed was my very worst time. He had on his old clothes, and he was tired. The police held a gun on him and everything. He had to go to jail for a few hours. I was sooo afraid he'd have to stay forever. It seemed like forever. Mom prayed he'd get out fast, and he did. But it didn't seem fast to me." Her voice dropped to a whisper. "Sometimes I dream he's in jail, and I wake up crying. When that happens I pray, then go to sleep again."

Just then Kathy saw the office door open. Her heart lodged in her throat. "They're coming out," she said hoarsely. Slowly she stood. Her legs shook so badly she plopped back in her chair.

Dad glanced toward the alcove and saw her. He smiled and led Brody and Duke down the hall. Linda and Steve hurried back to the party.

"The little red pills they said were drugs were little candies," Dad said. "Someone was playing a wicked trick on Brody. Steve said he'd make the announcement right now."

Kathy sighed in relief. She smiled at Brody and Duke, then at the Best Friends.

Dad pulled Brody close to his side. "We're all going back to the party, and we're going to have fun."

Kathy hesitated. Could she face all of them?

Brody lifted his chin and squared his shoulders. "I know I don't do drugs. I want the others to know too, so I want to stay."

"Then I'll go with you." Kathy stood beside Brody. "We'll all go in together!" This was her brother, and she would stay at his side!

13

Justine

Wednesday morning Kathy pushed Megan on the swing. She giggled and kicked her feet. Kathy pushed her again and again. Kathy had tried to get out of coming to the park this morning so she could see if Steve Perry called about last night's problem, but Mom said she had to take her little sister to the park. She wanted to know who'd done such a terrible thing to Brody. Dad said they might never learn the truth, but Steve was going to try.

"Stop me, Kathy!" Megan looked over her shoulder at Kathy. "Polly's here. I want to play with her."

Kathy caught the swing and stopped Megan in midair. Megan jumped out of the swing and ran over to Polly. They talked together, then ran to the sandbox. With a sigh Kathy walked to the park bench. Mike had been able to stay only a short time to help her practice. His mom was taking him shopping for school clothes. He hated shopping. Kathy chuckled. She'd rather be shopping than sitting in the park watching Megan play.

"Kathy?"

She jumped, then looked back to see Justine standing under a tree, her hands in the pockets of her jeans. Slowly Kathy stood and walked to Justine. "What's wrong?"

Justine brushed a tear off her cheek. "I'm so scared! I think my mom and dad are going to get a divorce."

"Oh, Justine! I'm sorry! But maybe you're wrong."

"I wish!" Justine slowly walked to the bench and sat down.

Kathy perched on the edge. A squirrel chattered from the top of a tree. Laughing and shouting, some kids ran from the slide to the merry-go-round. A truck drove past, leaving behind the smell of diesel fuel. Kathy turned to Justine. "Is that why you didn't stay at the party last night?"

Justine shrugged.

"Or was it because of Brody? They did prove he wasn't guilty. Those little red things really were candy."

"I know."

"Who told you?"

"Alyssa."

Kathy frowned. "But she wasn't even there."

"She talked Larry Roscoe into doing it to Brody. Larry thought it was only a joke. He'd never heard of Brody or his brother."

Kathy pressed her lips tightly together as anger rushed through her. She'd thought Alyssa wouldn't want to hurt Brody anymore. "Are you sure about this?"

Justine barely nodded. "I almost told you last night."

"You should've."

"I know." Justine looked down at the ground. The grass was rubbed off all along the front of the bench, leaving the sandy soil exposed. Ants scurried around, carrying food that had been dropped.

"Why didn't Larry tell what he'd done?"

Justine shrugged. "Scared like me probably."

Kathy watched Megan lean over and hug Polly.

"That's why Alyssa canceled practice yesterday . . . So you wouldn't see her and suspect something."

Kathy knotted her fists as fresh anger rushed through her. "She won't get away with this!"

"What are you going to do?"

"Tell my dad. He said the joke was too wicked to let pass. He said he'd talk to the person who dropped the candies. Now he'll want to talk to Alyssa . . . and probably her mom and dad."

"Please don't tell anyone I told." Justine shivered. "I don't want your dad yelling at me."

Kathy could see the fear in Justine's eyes and

finally nodded. "He wouldn't yell at you, but I won't tell."

"Thanks. I know I can trust you."

Kathy remembered she'd told the Best Friends about Justine's parents' fighting, and her heart sank. She had to tell Justine the truth even though it was hard to do. She took a deep breath. "I did something you won't like, Justine."

"What?" she asked in alarm.

"I told Hannah, Roxie, and Chelsea about your folks without thinking you wouldn't want it told."

Justine pressed her hands to her burning cheeks. "That's awful! Mom and Dad would hate to have others know! They told me lots of times to keep family things secret."

"I'm really sorry. But if they get a divorce, it'll all be out in the open anyway."

Justine's lip quivered. "Please *please* pray they won't get a divorce!"

"I will."

"I lay awake at night thinking about who I'd live with. I don't want to decide! I want them both!"

"I could ask my mom and dad to talk to yours."

"No! They'd be so embarrassed!"

"Then what can anybody do? What can *I* do?"

"I guess just listen to me." Justine darted a look at Kathy. "And be my friend."

"Sure. I can do that."

"I know you're good friends with Roxie and Hannah and the girl from Oklahoma."

"We said we'd never shut out new friends."

"I was afraid you would." Justine nervously rubbed the back of her hand. "Alyssa said you were only pretending to be my friend because of the cheerleading team."

Kathy frowned. "Alyssa's wrong! Maybe she acts that way, but I don't."

"I guess I know that."

They sat in silence a long time. Kathy squirmed uneasily. What could she say? She ran her hands down the legs of her jeans, then tugged at the collar of her pink T-shirt.

"I have to get back home." Justine slowly stood. "Thanks, Kathy."

"What did I do?" Shrugging, Kathy stood beside Justine.

"You listened to me. And you said you'd pray."

"I will too."

"I know." Justine brushed a tear off her tanned cheek. "When I start to feel bad, I know you're praying for me. It really helps."

"I'm glad." Kathy twisted her toe in the grass. "I asked Chelsea, Roxie, and Hannah to pray too. I hope you don't mind."

Justine shrugged. "I guess not. I'll see you this afternoon at Alyssa's."

"Unless she cancels again after my dad talks to her," Kathy said grimly.

"You'll think I'm awful, Kathy, but I don't want anything to keep me from getting on the cheerleading team."

"Neither do I, but we can't let Alyssa ruin Brody's reputation."

"You sure have changed toward him."

Kathy grinned. "I'm glad too. He's my brother, and I have to look out for him just like I do Duke and Megan."

"Even if you never make the team?"

Kathy hesitated. "I could have both."

"Maybe." Justine smiled. "See ya later."

"Later." Kathy watched Justine run out of the park. Silently she prayed for Justine and her parents.

Later Kathy walked Megan home, turned on the TV so Megan could watch the special Gospel Bill video, then hurried to the kitchen. Dad was drinking a cup of hot chocolate. It was his morning off. Kathy sat across from him and told him what Justine had said about Larry Roscoe and Alyssa.

Dad pushed back his chair. "I'll take care of it right now. I won't be gone long. Will you stay with Megan until I get back from seeing Alyssa?"

"Sure." Kathy ran to Dad and hugged him. He smelled like chocolate. How glad she was for a dad who listened to her and helped her! She knew kids at school who never talked to their dads or moms. She could talk to both, and they actually listened.

Kathy stood in the open door and watched Dad walk out of the yard. A warm breeze blew against her. A car drove past and honked. Dad waved at the driver of the car.

Just then the phone rang, and Kathy hurried to answer it. It was Chelsea.

"Can you work for Mrs. Carroll again today, Kath?"

She bit her lip and gripped the receiver. "I don't know. When?"

"This afternoon at 2."

"At 2! But that's when we have cheerleading practice."

"Maybe it's canceled—like yesterday."

Kathy frowned. "Something's going on. I'll find out and call you back."

"I told Mrs. Carroll somebody would work. She said she wanted *you*."

Kathy twisted the white phone cord. "She knows about practice, Chel."

"How about if I call her back and say you can work at 4?"

"Great. Then call me right back." Kathy hung up and paced the kitchen while she waited for Chelsea to call back. Maybe Mrs. Carroll would be talking with Dad and Alyssa.

The phone rang, and Kathy jumped. She answered it, and her voice cracked.

"Kathy, she said 4 was fine. I said you'd be there."

"Okay."

"I have to go, Kath. Talk to you later."

"Bye." Kathy hung up thoughtfully, then slowly walked to the window and looked out. Maybe she was making a mystery out of nothing.

The kitchen door opened, and she spun around. It was Dad.

"Nobody was home," he said.

Kathy gasped. "But that can't be!" She told Dad about Chelsea's call. "So I know she's home."

"That's strange. I think I'll go right back over there and try again."

"Maybe Alyssa saw you and wouldn't answer the door."

"Then I'll call first." Dad looked the number up and dialed it.

Kathy leaned weakly against the counter. Her nerves tightened even more when Dad started talking to Mrs. Carroll.

"I need to talk to Alyssa about Brody."

Kathy chewed her thumbnail.

"I'd like to come right now. Is Alyssa home?" Dad nodded to Kathy as he listened. "Good. I'll be right there." He hung up and tugged Kathy's curl. "You were right—Alyssa was home but didn't answer the door. Her mother doesn't know that. I'll be back as soon as possible."

Kathy wanted to beg him to take her along, but she didn't. It was soooo hard to wait!

After Dad left, Megan ran into the kitchen. Kathy sat her at the table to color in her new coloring book.

Megan looked up with a pleading look. "Color with me, Kathy."

"For a minute." Kathy sat at the table and colored a dog. She gave it purple spots, making Megan giggle.

Someone knocked on the back door, and Kathy hurried to answer it. Alyssa stood there, her face pale.

"My dad went to your house to talk to you," Kathy said sharply.

"I know. I slipped out and hid, then came here." Alyssa took a deep, shuddering breath. "Can I come in?"

"No!" Kathy stepped outdoors. "You talk to my dad. He wants to talk to you about Brody. Dad knows you had Larry Roscoe do that trick with the red candies last night. That was mean, Alyssa."

She hung her head. "I know . . . I'm sorry."

"Then why'd you do it?"

"I planned it before Tuesday night . . . Before I talked to Brody." Alyssa traced a crack in the sidewalk with her toe. "I tried to stop Larry, but he thought it was a good joke, so he said he was going to do it anyway."

"Why didn't you warn us?"

"I was too ashamed."

She looked like she meant it, but Kathy didn't trust her. "Why wouldn't you talk to my dad?"

Alyssa hung her head. "I just couldn't face him."

"He won't beat you or yell at you. He only wanted to tell you to leave Brody alone."

"I'm going to." Alyssa crossed her arms tightly. "But I can't face your dad. I just can't!"

Kathy shook her head. "He's determined to talk to you, so you might as well get it over with."

"No . . . please *please.*"

"What's wrong, Alyssa?" Kathy saw her fear, but she wasn't about to let Alyssa off again.

Alyssa was quiet a long time. She flicked a tear off her cheek. "My dad said if I do anything more to cause trouble for anyone, he'll make me quit cheerleading. I just can't do that! You know how important it is to me."

"I do understand, but you should've left Brody alone."

"I know." Alyssa twisted her fingers. "He won't talk to my mom if I'm not there, will he?"

"He might."

Alyssa groaned.

"But if he talks to you alone, you could settle the problem without your folks knowing."

"Really? Would your dad do that?"

"Yes. He's nice."

"Like you."

Kathy smiled.

Alyssa rubbed her hands up and down her arms as if to warm herself. "Are you sure your dad won't tell mine?"

"If you ask him not to, he won't." Kathy wagged her finger at Alyssa. "But you can't keep doing bad things to Brody."

"I won't. I promise." Alyssa wiped a tear off her cheek. "Can I come in and wait for him?"

"Sure." Kathy led the way to the kitchen. "Sit down and color a picture with Megan."

"Yes, do!" Megan bounced up and down.

"Are you kidding?"

Kathy sat beside Megan and looked up at Alyssa. "Don't you do that with your brother and sister?"

"No way!"

"Kathy colored this one." Megan touched a picture. "And Brody did this, and Duke did this one. And Dad did this, and Mom did this."

"That's enough, Megan," Kathy said with a laugh.

Alyssa sank to the edge of a chair. "I never

thought about doing anything with Mark and Tammy."

"You should. It's fun."

Megan kept coloring, looking at Kathy and Alyssa as they talked.

Alyssa touched the crayons. "Your family does a lot of things together, don't they?"

Kathy nodded. "We like it that way."

Alyssa picked up a red crayon and colored a bow around a kitten's neck. "I haven't colored for a long time."

"You can color with me anytime you want," Megan said, smiling.

"Thanks."

Kathy watched them color together as they waited for Dad. When he came, Alyssa's face paled.

Dad looked stern. "Come to my study, Alyssa."

Kathy touched his arm. "Dad, I told her you wouldn't tell her folks on her as long as she leaves Brody alone."

"Please, Mr. Aber! Please don't tell them."

He sighed and nodded. "But we're going to have a very serious talk, young lady."

Kathy watched them walk away. Knowing Dad would take care of everything, she smiled and turned back to Megan to color in her book.

14

Cheerleaders

With a shout Kathy leaped high, then flipped across Alyssa's yard. She heard the others clapping and cheering. With one last mighty flip, she landed inches from Sharon. Kathy's hair was damp with sweat. Her hands were green from grass stains. Smiling, her chest rose and fell.

"That was great!" they all said at once.

"Can you teach me to do flips?" Alyssa asked eagerly.

"Sure." Kathy smiled. She was glad Alyssa had talked to Dad earlier and settled everything. She seemed relaxed and didn't snap at them like she had before.

"How can we use the flips and cartwheels in our yells?" Debbie asked.

Kathy told them about a yell she'd made up.

"That's great!" Laughing, Justine clapped her hands. "I can do a cartwheel."

Kathy smiled at Justine. She was happier than she'd been this morning in the park. Kathy planned to ask her about that in private later.

"Teach us your yell," Alyssa said.

Kathy quickly agreed. She worked with the girls a while until they all did cartwheels at the right time. At the end of the yell Kathy did three forward flips, then three backward ones.

"That's a great yell," Debbie said with a laugh.

"Okay, girls . . ." Alyssa took a deep breath.

Kathy tensed. Was Alyssa going to get bossy again?

"I have a surprise for you." Smiling, Alyssa waved toward the house.

Holding her breath, Kathy watched the red door open. Alyssa's aunt walked out, smiling and waving. She was short and slight with long blonde hair and big blue eyes.

Kathy sucked in her breath as she recognized Pamela Brewer. What was Alyssa up to this time?

Alyssa slipped her arm around the woman. "Girls, this is my aunt. I told her about you, Kathy." Alyssa bit her lip and blushed. "I was wrong about her, Aunt Pamela. She has a good attitude. And she'd make a great cheerleader."

"I can see that for myself. You are *all* good. I like the way you work together."

Smiling, Kathy relaxed. Mrs. Brewer had seen her and judged her on her work, not on Alyssa's word! "I'm glad you happened to be here today," Kathy said.

"Oh, I didn't just happen to be here." Mrs. Brewer looped her fingers in her jeans. "Alyssa invited me to come watch all of you. She said I'd be impressed, and I most certainly am."

Kathy smiled at Alyssa. While Mrs. Brewer was talking to the girls Kathy whispered, "Thanks, Alyssa."

"I wanted to do something nice for you. If I could do something nice for Brody, I would."

"Just be his friend. He'd like that."

"I'll try. And I'll see if the other girls will too."

"Good."

"Okay, girls, let me see some more of your cheers," Mrs. Brewer said as she sat on the steps and wrapped her arms around her knees.

Kathy smiled at the girls as they got in line the way Alyssa told them to.

Later at home Kathy ran to the study to tell Mom what had happened. She wasn't there, but Brody was. He was looking in the top drawer of the desk again. Kathy's heart dropped to her feet. She was afraid to say anything, but she just had to ask. "What are you doing, Brody?"

He jumped and slammed the drawer shut.

"Well? What are you doing?"

He flushed to the roots of his hair.

She jabbed her finger at him. "You know you aren't supposed to do that!"

"I know." Brody slowly stood. "I want my mom's phone number, so I can call her."

Kathy stared at him a long time. Was that all he wanted? "Why didn't you just ask for it?"

He frowned. "Your folks don't want me calling her."

"Did they say that?"

"No."

"Then ask them." Kathy spread her hands. "They'll let you call."

Brody sighed heavily. "Why should they let me? Why be so nice to me?"

"Because they love you."

Brody's chin quivered. "Really? I can't believe it."

"Believe it! Really. Come on, we'll get the phone number and you can call your mom." Kathy started for the door and stopped to look back at him. "Brody, I saw you going through the desk the other day. Were you looking for her phone number then too?"

He nodded. "I wanted to go live with her. That's when I thought you hated me."

Kathy flushed. "I'm sorry, Brody."

"I know better now." He rubbed a hand over his eyes. "I miss my mom a lot. I didn't think I would, but . . . she's my mom."

"I understand." Kathy smiled and hurried to find her mother. She was in Megan's bedroom, sitting in the rocking chair with Megan on her lap, reading her a story.

"Want to listen to the story?" Megan asked, smiling.

"Sure," Kathy said as she dropped to the floor beside the red plastic toybox.

Brody nodded as he sank to the edge of the bed.

Mom smiled and finished the story. She gave Megan the book to put back on the shelf and looked from Kathy to Brody. "Now, what do you really want?"

"Ask Brody," Kathy said.

"Well?"

Brody slowly stood. "I want to call my mom." He swallowed hard. "Is that all right?"

"Of course." Mom slipped her arm around Brody's shoulders. "I wrote the number inside the kitchen phone book for you. I thought I told you."

Brody shook his head. "You didn't. Can I call now?"

"Sure. Tell her we're glad to have you here with us."

"Tell her we like having another brother." Kathy smiled.

"I like having a whole family," Brody said hoarsely. Flushing, he ran to the kitchen.

Mom hugged Kathy. "I'm glad you got your feelings settled with each other."

"Me too." Kathy hugged Mom tightly. "I love you, Mom."

Later Kathy sat in her backyard with the Best Friends. She'd told them all that had happened. "It's really exciting to solve mysteries and settle problems."

"Now we have a wedding to go to." Roxie sighed heavily. "You have a new brother, Kathy, and I'm getting a new grandpa."

"You'll learn to love him," Hannah said. "He's nice."

"I think the *King's Kids* should buy them a wedding gift." Chelsea looked at the girls. "If you agree, raise your hand."

Laughing, Kathy lifted her arm high along with the others. "We really do have a business meeting every time we get together."

Chelsea grinned sheepishly. "That's not all. Ezra called me to ask if the *King's Kids* could watch his place and take care of his lawn while they're on their honeymoon. I said we would."

"What about Gracie? Or are they taking the dog with them?" Hannah asked.

Chelsea giggled and leaned toward Roxie. "Guess who's going to take care of Gracie?"

Shaking her head, Roxie jumped up. "Not me! Oh no, you don't—not me!"

Chelsea laughed. "Nope. Mike!"

Kathy tipped back her head and laughed. She listened to the laughter of the Best Friends, and her heart almost burst with happiness. Just then she caught a movement inside the house. She saw Brody standing there watching them. She waved at him, and he smiled and waved back, then slipped into the music room.

"Girls, want to hear my new brother play the guitar?"

"Yes!" they all cried together.

Kathy led the way, and they all pushed into the music room to listen to Brody.

You are invited to become a *Best Friends Member!*

In becoming a member you'll receive a club membership card with your name on the front and a list of the Best Friends and their favorite Bible verses on the back along with a space for your favorite Scripture. You'll also receive a colorful, 2-inch, specially-made I'M A BEST FRIEND button and a write-up about the author, Hilda Stahl, with her autograph. As a bonus you'll get an occasional newsletter about the upcoming BEST FRIENDS books.

All you need to do is mail your NAME, ADDRESS (printed neatly, please), AGE and $3.00 for postage and handling to:

BEST FRIENDS
P.O. Box 96
Freeport, MI 49325

WELCOME TO THE CLUB!

(Authorized by the author, Hilda Stahl)